A RELIC OF WAR

Mordecai Ledbury, the most famous advocate of his day and a man with many enemies, spends a night in a dilapidated old family house, hoping to discover what event in her early life had turned his mother into such an embittered woman. By morning, a masked intruder lies dead, shot with a pistol which is a relic of Mordecai's eccentric uncle. Mordecai admits to firing the shot, so is he guilty of murder or was it a tragic accident? A dark family secret and a courtroom drama combine to make this a gripping legal cliffhanger.

A RELIC OF WAR

by

Peter Rawlinson

Magna Large Print Books
Long Preston, North Yorkshire,
BD23 4ND, England.

British Library Cataloguing in Publication Data.

Rawlinson, Peter
    A relic of war.

    A catalogue record of this book is
    available from the British Library

    ISBN   0-7505-2334-4

First published in Great Britain 2004 by Constable,
an imprint of Constable & Robinson Ltd.

Published in Large Print 2005 by arrangement with
Constable & Robinson Ltd.

Magna Large Print is an imprint of Library Magna Books Ltd.

Printed and bound in Great Britain by
T.J. (International) Ltd., Cornwall, PL28 8RW

Prologue

He was standing at the top of the staircase looking like a prophet of old with his scarred face and his white beard and long white hair when the beam of the torch from the hall below lit his face. He had turned from the door to his bedroom when he heard the shattering of the glass of the window in the room below.

He came from the library where he had been sitting in the dark, resting his one tired and failing eye, thinking as always about Anne. It was over a quarter of a century since she had been killed and he had fled from the hospital where they were about to treat his wounded, mutilated face and had come home. To live thereafter the solitary life of a recluse. The light from the torch below blinded him. He put his hand to his face to shield his one eye from the light and tried to switch on the torch he was carrying but failed. Suddenly a searing pain like the thrust of a knife pierced his chest. He bent forward, crumpling, the torch falling from his hand. He swayed – and then fell, at first face forward, then tumbling, turning over and over like a rag doll until he came to rest at the foot of the stairs spread-eagled at the feet of the masked man.

The man turned his torch on to the figure by his feet, lighting the distorted, obviously broken neck, the scarred, livid face, now bloodied by a great gash on the temple, the single eye staring vacantly upward, the other an empty socket since the eye-patch had been torn away by the fall. The stump of the left arm protruded through a gash in the shirt, it too pouring blood.

The man in the mask drew in his breath and stepped back. Then he switched off his torch and ran to the front door, tearing back the bolts, struggling with the great key in the lock, wrenching it open, and leaving it open behind him, letting in the moonlight. The man ran across the drive and plunged into a bank of overgrown laurel and rhododendron. When the sound of his footsteps on the gravel and the crash of his body as he ran through the shrubbery had died, and when far off the sound of the car being driven away had faded, nothing broke the silence. The dead man lay, his neck broken, near the table on which that day he had placed fresh wild flowers in the bowl, his daily tribute to his long-dead love.

Whenever the clouds passed from the face of the moon, the light filtered through the open door into the hall and lit up his face. He seemed to be smiling.

Chapter One

1

No man and certainly no woman ever denied Aaron Ledbury's beguiling charm, not even those whom he had enticed, to their subsequent regret, into various unfortunate enterprises as financial partners. For none of these disasters was he ever personally blamed. By all those who knew him he was liked, and by many he was loved.

In appearance he was striking – very tall, rather stooped, with thinning hair even in youth and, in consequence of this, an imposing expanse of forehead and brow. His eyes were dark brown and very expressive, his nose rather fleshy and his smile, which revealed gold teeth, attractive. His voice was especially melodious, with a faint hint of some foreign intonation.

Nominally he appeared to be a partner in a firm of stockbrokers. He played poker and bridge, the poker professionally, the bridge socially, winning and losing with style and grace. He was interested in horses, not to ride but to watch and to back, and it was when he came north to York races in the

August of 1909 that he met Grace Fairbairn. He was forty-five; she just two days past her twenty-first birthday. The second child of her family, born many years after an elder brother, she had been brought up, she told him, at the family home, Water Meadow House, Kingsford Langley in Dorset, but she had fallen out with her family and had no wish to see any of them again. At the time when she met Aaron, she was strikingly pretty, fairly short with a full figure, an abundance of blonde hair, good features, a slightly too prominent nose and piercing blue eyes. She herself had not come to York for the races. She had joined the house party, uninvited by host or hostess, at the behest of Sophie, the daughter of the house. After Aaron had spent some time chatting with her, using all his charm to draw her out, he was surprised and amused by the directness with which she expressed her opinions and by the dogmatic certainty with which she held them. But despite her good looks she was, he thought, much like the daughter of a friend whose mother described her as having 'come from the womb angry'.

She was, he discovered, financially independent, having inherited some money from a relative, and she had been studying painting in watercolour at the Royal Academy Schools in London. Aaron was greatly taken by her. She told him that soon after her arrival in London in 1907, she had fallen out with the elderly cousin with whom she was supposed to board and had moved to other lodgings, passing her time when not at the Schools with her fellow students in the tearooms and restaurants and even the public houses of Piccadilly. Quite the emancipated, twentieth-century young woman, she described the celebration of her twenty-first birthday, passed in an attic apartment in Bedford Square with a dozen of her fellow students drinking burgundy at half-a-crown a bottle – and a flask of absinthe provided by Sophie's young man. They had played the pianoforte, sung music hall songs and danced. Dawn had found them squatting on the floor drinking cups of cocoa laced with the absinthe. From Sophie's home in York, she and Sophie and Sophie's young man planned to set out with some other friends on a bicycling and painting holiday along the west coast of Scotland.

Their arrival at Sophie's parents' rambling, redbrick house near York had caused consternation. Sophie's father, a retired Commander in the Royal Navy, was put out. He did not think they would 'fit in' with the party of racegoers. The newcomers, his wife had to explain apologetically to the other guests, were 'artistic'. The host and hostess, however, need not have worried. Aaron Ledbury took charge of the new arrivals. He was particularly attentive to Grace Fairbairn, even managing to be polite and friendly with Sophie's young man who, to the Commander's disgust, appeared at dinner in his velvet jacket and flowing black cravat.

At the end of dinner when the ladies had retired leaving the men to drink their port and discuss form for the races next day, Aaron drew up his chair beside that of the young student, sought his opinion of the Impressionists, discussed with him Degas and Berthe Morisot, and enquired the route in Scotland that the bicycling group intended to follow. He then suggested certain hotels where they should stay. When the men rejoined the ladies in the drawing room, he sat himself down beside Grace Fairbairn.

Later, when the bicycling party arrived at each of the hotels in the Highlands that Aaron had suggested, they found wine and flowers – all addressed to Miss Fairbairn, accompanied by a note.

'He's twenty years older than you,' Sophie protested to Grace.

But just twenty days after they had first met, Aaron Ledbury and Grace Fairbairn eloped.

2

They were married in Paris. From the Ritz

Grace wrote a curt note to her family announcing her marriage. The following day the Ledburys left for Nice and the Canton Hotel.

Grace was in a state of utter sensual ecstasy. She could not wait to be alone with her husband, primarily in bed. Aaron was flattered by her enjoyment of his experienced lovemaking. Each morning in Nice they rose late and he escorted her to different couturiers and jewellers and perfumiers. Each evening after they had dined he took her for a stroll along the Promenade des Anglais before leading her into the casino where they passed hour after hour at the baccarat table, Aaron playing, she at his side. She did not understand the game but was content to sit at the table, never taking her eyes off her husband. On the first evening, from where she lay in bed, she saw him in the dressing room laying out 500 franc notes one by one on the dresser. But this was not repeated on the two subsequent evenings. On these evenings his piles of brightly coloured chips swiftly diminished and then disappeared, until replaced in response to Aaron's scribbled notes. When finally the chips had all disappeared and no more notes from Aaron were forthcoming, he took her back to their suite in the Carlton Hotel where he made love to her and was as sweet-tempered and loving as he had been when they had dined so happily in the grill room.

Next morning Aaron announced that they were moving on, and that afternoon they caught the slow train along the coast and through the tunnels to Rapallo. It was when they were dining in the Hotel Splendide on the evening of their arrival that Aaron was brought a telegram. For a moment a brief cloud passed over his face; then it went. But the following morning they were on the express to Paris, and from there boarded the boat train to Calais, Dover and London. At Victoria station he told her he had pressing business in the City and hurried away in a hansom, leaving her to make her way in a separate cab to the furnished rooms he had taken for them unseen, in Maida Vale.

After a month, Grace pointed out to her husband the shabbiness of the apartment in which they were living. He said he had not noticed, but the next evening he announced that he had been lent a villa in St John's Wood belonging to a friend who had recently moved to the United States. Although Grace had not seen it, he was sure she would approve. Ten days later, they moved in.

Fourteen months from the date of their marriage, on a dark and cool October morning in 1910, in the principal bedroom of the villa that was still being 'lent' by its absentee owner, and after an uncomfortable pregnancy and a lengthy and painful labour,

Grace was delivered of a boy. The birth had been supervised by a friend of Aaron's who although inconveniently practising in Bromley, Aaron had insisted should look after Grace while she was pregnant. He was giving his services free, in exchange for a debt at poker.

As soon as the doctor handed Grace the baby and she saw the head, larger than normal as it seemed to her and covered in dark hair, and the small, deformed feet, she shuddered and turned her face away. Despite the cajoling of Aaron and the nurse, she refused to take him into her arms, neither then nor in the weeks and months that followed. Instead it was Aaron who took the child, crooning to him as he walked up and down the room. It was the start of a lifelong love between father and son.

'Mordecai,' Aaron said of his son. 'We shall call him Mordecai.'

As it had begun, so it went on, Grace rejecting the baby, refusing to have anything to do with him, leaving all his nurture and attention to the nurse. When Aaron gently chided her, she replied that the child was ugly and a cripple. In private she called him a monster. And with the baby's arrival, the passion that had blazed between Aaron and Grace during those first months of the marriage ended and was never regained. It had brought Grace a joy she had not thought possible. For what she had lost, she blamed her son.

3

Happily for the Ledbury family the return from America of the owner of the villa in St John's Wood coincided with a swing in Aaron's fortunes, and in May 1914 he bought a large three-storey house in Tregunter Road in Chelsea. By then Mordecai was three, a strange, alert little boy, highly intelligent, with a large, domed head, who stumped about as well as he could on his deformed feet, often falling but always refusing to cry. He was looked after by an Irish nanny, Maisie, whom he adored.

Every day she took him to Kensington Gardens, and tried to protect him when he limped along to join other children playing with their boats on the Round Pond. They would push him away and he'd fall and Maisie would run to him and scream at the other children. 'Get away, ye little brutes, leave him alone. Can't ye see he has the bad legs, ye little divils?' She'd lift him up into her arms and carry him away across the grass, leaving the other children frightened and resentful. Their nannies would tell Maisie she shouldn't bring her child here if he was unable to play and to mind her temper, adding when she was out of earshot that the child was a nasty little dwarf with his large head and horrid face; he was enough to scare anyone, let alone children.

At night in the nursery, with the night lamp burning in a corner casting a shadow on the ceiling, Mordecai would lie awake, knowing that he was different, that other children disliked and despised him. His mother, unable to hide her revulsion, was a rare visitor to the nursery on the top of the house. Aaron came more often, bringing with him fun and noise and laughter, the scent of cigars and, as Maisie noted reproachfully, brandy. But he brought presents, boxes of lead soldiers or a tin clockwork train, and he would march round the nursery with a towel wrapped round his head singing the latest music hall song with Mordecai perched on his shoulders and Maisie by the door, giggling. Mordecai loved him desperately and longed for him to come more often. But not his mother. Mordecai was frightened of his mother. Once she had lost her temper and struck him. He had been allowed into her studio and when she had been distracted by a servant asking for instructions he had dabbled his hand in her palette and dripped paint on to her painting book. She had boxed his ears and slapped his face and he was forbidden ever to come near her studio again. But sometimes he'd stand by the conservatory door looking into the studio – and hating.

Three months after they had moved into Tregunter Road the Great War began – and later came the Zeppelins. Mordecai enjoyed the nights when Maisie carried him down to the basement where the whole household was assembled in their dressing gowns. He'd stare with the large, dark eyes he'd inherited from his father at Grace sitting in her chair surrounded by the servant maids and clutching a bottle of smelling salts.

Aaron was rarely with them. He had joined the Observer Corps and appeared in the nursery in his uniform, a serge naval-style jacket and a peaked cap. Occasionally he was on duty at a searchlight post in Hyde Park, for which he prepared by loading his pockets with a flask of brandy and cigars; on other nights he was just not at home. Where he was, Grace no longer asked or cared. Aaron sometimes hired a gallery and put on a show for her, but her watercolours of flowers and *nature morte* were too pretty for the wartime mood and few were sold. She tried to ignore the war and never glanced at the newspapers with their ever-lengthening casualty lists. She told Aaron she was not even interested in the fate of her soldier brother.

When he was five, Mordecai was sent to a smart private infants' school in Kensington Square where he was taken and collected by

Maisie. He was quick and sharp, absorbing everything he was taught. He'd learnt to read very early but his handwriting was an almost indecipherable scrawl, as though his mind worked too fast for his hand. But during playtime he stood alone, leaning against a door as he watched the other children running about in the garden behind the school.

In 1918, when he was eight and the war came to an end, he left the infants' school and went to a daytime preparatory school in the Cromwell Road. Here he was mocked, called 'Big Head' and 'Stump Foot' and pushed over and jeered at when he tried to get to his feet. But in class he was always the first – and was mocked all the more for that.

In 1921, with the post-war boom over, there came another swing in Aaron's fortunes, this time sharply downward. Tregunter Road was sold, the servants dismissed and the family moved south of the river to a small brick house in Lambeth. Maisie stayed on for some months, sharing a small bedroom with Mordecai, until one day she announced that she was going back to Ireland. Mordecai, she said, was too old now to share a room with her. As her suitcase was strapped into the compartment in the taxi beside the driver, Mordecai was given a warm, tear-stained embrace. He remained on the doorstep as the cab trundled off towards the river and on to Euston station where Maisie would catch the Irish Mail for Holyhead and the crossing to the newly named Dun Laoghaire – or Kingstown as Maisie still called it. Mordecai was alone now. He went back into the house, climbed the stairs into his room and lay on the bed, dry-eyed.

Since the departure from Tregunter Road, Grace, still only in her thirties, had grown ever more peevish, embittered by the loss of her fine house and studio. Her blonde hair had already faded and become prematurely streaked with white. Her face grew pinched. She looked more like a woman of fifty, while the new conditions in which she was forced to live in closer proximity to her son, drove her more and more into herself. For hours she lay on her bed with a bottle of sal volatile in her hand, or disappeared for long walks in the shabby Lambeth streets.

Aaron, however, now in his fifties and with what little hair remained to him restricted to two small patches on the side of his head above his prominent ears, remained as cheerful and irrepressible as ever.

'One day,' he assured Grace, 'our ship will come in. Soon things will get better. I am sure of it.'

It was all right for him, Grace would reply. He wasn't cooped up in that horrid little hovel for hours and hours on end. And it was all right for the boy too, she added. (She

18

rarely called him Mordecai.) He was away all day at school. Only she suffered from the wretched life Aaron's failure imposed upon them.

Sometimes, during these years, she thought of her family and the home in Dorset that she had left. But they were not kind thoughts. She was so consumed with hatred for her parents and her brother that she'd rather starve before she ever turned to them. She read in the newspaper that her brother had married. She read of the death of her mother, then of her father. But she did not write – and she certainly did not visit. She refused, as she had always refused, to discuss with Aaron the reason for her loathing.

Then, one Monday evening in 1923, Aaron returned home early. He called Mordecai down from his homework in his bedroom and perched Grace on a chair in the small sitting room. She sat looking at him with pursed lips, waiting for the announcement of yet another disaster. Mordecai stood in a corner of the room, away from his mother, leaning against the wall. Aaron had a bowler hat in his hand behind his back. Now he put it on, tilting it a racy angle and began to sing.

'I walked along the Bois de Boolong, I heard them all declare, He must be a millionaire, the man who broke the bank at Monte Carlo.'

Grace looked at him stonily; Mordecai

began to grin.

'You will be pleased to learn,' Aaron began, addressing his wife, 'that this afternoon I have taken a lease on a large apartment in a modern mansion block in Cheyne Walk overlooking the river. We shall be moving within the week. No more will we have to live in this hovel as you have so rightly called it. From now on we shall be in a fine apartment on the first floor of a modern building with four bedrooms, of which the one with the north light will be immediately converted into a studio.'

At this Grace looked up.

'We shall have a fine drawing room with a view over the river,' Aaron went on, 'and a large dining room eminently suitable for Mr and Mrs Ledbury to entertain in style. There'll be a study for myself, a large bedroom for Master Ledbury and a room off the kitchen for a maid. There is a lift; there is even a porter. And you,' he said to Mordecai, 'will go to St Paul's in Hammersmith where you will mix with the smartest minds of your generation.' He raised his bowler hat. 'A new life is starting. Now the sun will never stop shining.' He picked Grace up from the chair and began to waltz her around the room, singing 'The Man Who Broke The Bank', looking over her shoulder at Mordecai and winking. Despite herself Grace began to smile. But not for long.

'Stop it, you silly old fool,' she said, 'you'll have a heart attack.'

But he whirled her on and on until, exhausted, he flopped on to the sofa, his bowler hat rolling along the carpet until it came to rest by the black medical boots of his son.

4

Aaron lay dying in the second best bedroom in Cheyne Walk where the family had now lived for nearly a decade. Grace occupied the best, next to her studio. A week earlier he had suffered a stroke when he was playing bridge at the Marlborough-Wyndham club. He fell across the table, the cards fluttering from his hands, and they took him to St George's Hospital at Hyde Park Corner. His first words when he regained consciousness were, 'It was such a very good hand.'

He had a second stroke that night and the doctors told Mordecai that they could do nothing for him. He was, after all, almost seventy. It was best to take him home.

In Cheyne Walk Mordecai drew up his chair close beside the bed, for Aaron spoke with difficulty and his speech was slurred.

'My clever barrister son,' Aaron said fondly.

'Not quite a barrister, Father. I still have to be called.'

'When?'

'In October.'

'Then I shall not live to see it. But you are qualified?'

'I am.' He had come third in the whole list.

Aaron smiled. 'You have passed all your exams and you've eaten all your dinners?'

'I have.'

'A quaint custom that, eating your way into a profession.'

'And not particularly good eating. But you would have approved of the wine.'

'How old are you now?'

'Twenty-two.'

'You are losing your hair even earlier than I did.' Aaron put his hand on his son's face. Mordecai's hair was brushed left to right across his domed head, failing to conceal the bald patches. The two sticks with which he walked were leaning against the bottom of Aaron's bed. 'And your life away from the law? What is that?'

'Not much.'

'And love? Is there any love in your life? Have you lovers?'

'Only whores.'

Aaron sighed. 'That is a pity.'

'It is. But I am not exactly a beauty.'

'That does not matter. Looks do not matter, for a man. It is the voice that matters. You have a beautiful voice and it will serve you well in your profession.'

'It is your voice, Father.'

'Maybe. It is said that men are seduced by the eye; women by the ear. Remember that.'

A long silence followed. Then Aaron said, 'I wronged your mother by marrying her. She was too young...' He paused, as though struggling for the words. 'She was in fact experienced. She wanted to marry me and at first she doted on me. But I destroyed the spark of rebellion in her. I should never have married her.'

It was I who wronged her, thought Mordecai. I wronged her by being born. I killed her passion for her husband. And I shamed her by being born as I am.

'I thought she would not mind the uncertain existence that I led as much as she did,' Aaron went on. 'Those ups and downs that to me were the excitement, the essence of life. To her they were a crucifixion.'

He shut his eyes and again there was silence. When he opened his eyes he said, 'When I am gone there will be little money. Your mother will have to sell the lease of this apartment. She will get a good sum for it. Enough to buy something smaller and to have something left over. That and her own money should be enough. But she'll have to move again. She'll not like that. All her married life, she once said to me, she's been on the move.' He turned his head to look at Mordecai. 'She should approach her brother.'

'Her brother?'

'Yes, she has a brother, much older than she. She should approach him.'

'She has never spoken of him,' said Mordecai.

'No, and she never will approach him. She'll ask nothing of him. She cut herself off from the whole family. It had happened before we married. She hates them – why, I have never fathomed.' There was a minute of silence before the slurred voice continued, 'When I'm gone there'll be little for you, you know that?'

Mordecai nodded. 'I don't expect anything.' And he wouldn't go with his mother to wherever she went after she had sold Cheyne Walk. When Aaron was gone, he'd be gone. 'I'll manage,' he said.

Aaron suddenly stretched out his hand and took Mordecai's.

'We always got on well, you and me. Are you fond of me?'

'Of course. You know I am.'

'Fond enough to do me a favour?'

'Certainly. What favour?'

'It will have to be a secret between you and me. No one else, you understand?'

Mordecai nodded again.

'There is someone I need to see before I die.'

'You want someone to come and see you here?'

'Where else? I won't be moving – not until the men in black come with their wooden box.'

'Who is it you want to see?'

'Not the lawyer. I have done with him. And names do not matter. The name will mean nothing to you. What I want is for you to take your mother out – take her to luncheon, or a drive in the park or to the cinema. I need an hour when neither of you is here. The nurse will let in the visitor. I shall pay her to keep quiet. But there is not much time. Tomorrow you must do it, the next day at the very latest.'

'Is that the favour? Is that all you want me to do, just take Mother out?'

'When you have fixed the time when you and your mother will be out, tell me and I shall give you a telephone number to call. When your call is answered, you must merely say that I shall be expecting a visit at Cheyne Walk at the time you appoint. Nothing more. Do you understand?'

So it was arranged. There was an exhibition of watercolours, Mordecai told Grace, at the Royal Academy. She should see it. She needed to get out of the house for a break. He would take her. It would do her good. At first she demurred. She rarely went out alone with Mordecai. She did not like to be seen with him.

He pressed her, telling her that she really

should not miss the exhibition. It was of the finest of English watercolourists, her heroes, Cotman, Girtin, Crome and also many Turners. And it was shortly to close. She relented but when he said that they could have luncheon afterwards at the Criterion in Piccadilly Circus, she refused point blank. So he said that as they would be in the West End, did she not perhaps want to do some shopping? No, she would look at the pictures and then come home.

Twenty minutes to the Academy, he calculated. Say an hour looking at the pictures. Twenty minutes back. One hour and forty minutes. Allow an hour and a half. Aaron had said he needed an hour. It was the best Mordecai could do.

He telephoned the number Aaron had given him.

'This is Aaron Ledbury's son,' he began. 'From noon tomorrow my mother and I will be out for an hour. My father would welcome a visit.'

'Very well,' was the reply. The voice was rather high-pitched, with a faint Cockney accent. He tried to make her say more.

'You know the address?'

'I do. Thank you.' And she rang off.

Grace was not ready at noon. Mordecai had a taxi waiting at the front door. He hoped the woman would have wit enough to watch and see them get into the taxi and drive away before she came to the front door of the mansion block and rang their bell. She had – for no one had appeared before twelve minutes past noon when he and Grace drove away.

The traffic during the drive to Piccadilly was light, and what was worse, Grace declared she had a headache. So she did not linger in the gallery as long as he had hoped. Flower pictures are what I admire, she said. Mordecai had deliberately not ordered a taxi for their return, saying reasonably enough that he had not known when she would be ready to leave, and hoping that they would have difficulty finding one.

'You should have hired a car,' Grace said crossly.

'I'll look for a cab.'

'How can you possibly do that?' Grace said looking at his sticks. 'I'll go myself.'

He hobbled after her as she bustled across the front courtyard. At that moment a taxi turned in and deposited its passengers at the steps at the entrance to the Academy and was moving away. Grace hailed it. The cab stopped and Grace got in. Mordecai was, by then, near the statue of Joshua Reynolds in the centre of the courtyard. He took his time in joining her. When they started to drive back to Chelsea down Piccadilly, it was after one o'clock and the middle of the lunch hour rush. So it was half-past one when the cab, approaching down the Embankment from the east, did a U-turn and drew up in front of their block of flats. Grace did not notice, but Mordecai did, the tall, veiled figure hurrying away towards Chelsea Bridge. He stayed on the step looking after her, at the slim legs in their silk stockings and the faint glimpse of blonde hair beneath the black veil.

He went up to his father's room. 'We cut it rather fine,' he said.

'It was enough,' Aaron replied.

He died two days later. As he had warned Mordecai, there was little money. The whole estate amounted to £5000 cash and the twenty-year unexpired portion of the lease. But for Mordecai, to his surprise, there was a bequest of £1000 and his father's gold hunter with its heavy gold chain.

The money would keep him for two years, with prudence for three, until he started to earn at the bar.

The lease of the apartment was put on the market and sold well. Mordecai told Grace he would not be coming to live with her in her new flat. She made no protest. Nor did she ask where he intended to go.

The Anglican chapel at Putney Cemetery was crowded for Aaron had many friends. Mordecai had chosen the hymns, rousing hymns that he knew Aaron would have enjoyed: 'I vow to thee my country' and 'Jerusalem'. The congregation sang lustily.

Grace, who thought the music absurd, stood dry-eyed, perfectly composed. She followed the coffin to the grave, turning now and then to frown at Mordecai as he hobbled to keep up with her.

When she entered the chapel she had been too uninterested to notice a blonde woman accompanied by two small children. Now seated in the car and about to be driven away, she spotted the small group still hovering by the grave.

'Do you see that woman?' she asked Mordecai. 'What is she doing standing over the grave of your father?'

The car began to move. Nothing could harm Aaron now.

'She is, I believe,' Mordecai replied, 'a friend of my father's. And her children are my relatives.'

Chapter Two

1

Mr Justice Plumpton was inordinately proud of being a Justice of the High Court and he did not conceal it. He had an orotund style of speaking, an aldermanic belly to accompany the voice, and a deceptively benign face. It was deceptive because although in appearance he looked rather like a modern-day Mr Pickwick twinkling behind his half-moon glasses, he was the most unamiable of creatures and the most pompous of judges. During the summer assize of 1934 he had reached the ripe age of seventy-five but he had a life tenure as a High Court judge and had not the slightest intention of retiring. He was determined, as he put it, to soldier on, announcing that he still had ahead of him 'many years of useful service to give to the public'.

He preferred life on circuit away from London, travelling across the country to preside at the assize courts in various cities scattered across the counties of England and Wales. In the Royal Courts of Justice in the Strand in London he was surrounded by his contemporaries and equals and in close proximity to the Lord Chief Justice, the only authority of which he stood in awe. By contrast, out in the country, he was often the sole judge on an assize and able to lord it over everyone. He was also able to escape from his wife, Lady Plumpton, a tall beak-nosed woman who had bossed him about for thirty years and now found it difficult even to tolerate his presence near to her. Accordingly she encouraged him to be out of London during the law terms; during the shorter Law Vacations she paid visits to an old friend in Florence and during the Long Vacation in the summer to cousins in Maine in the United States.

The circuit Mr Justice Plumpton most enjoyed visiting was the Western, with its cathedral towns of Winchester, Salisbury, Exeter and sometimes Wells, and where the lodgings in which the Judge of Assize was quartered, at the local authority's expense, were usually handsome eighteenth-century or early Victorian buildings, fitting accommodation, he thought, for someone as important as he. For, as he continually reminded everyone, when in commission as the Judge of Assize, he was representing the Sovereign. The implication was clear. He expected to be treated as royalty, and indeed the wife of one Under-Sheriff, a permanent appointee who carried out all the actual shrieval business such as supervising the bailiffs, did once make him a kind of curtsey, at which he was gracious enough not to smile.

The judge may have liked the Western Circuit; but the circuit did not like the judge. In fact the circuit disliked him intensely. This was principally true of the barrister circuiteers and the local solicitors who practised in the courts in the West Country, for on the bench Mr Justice Plumpton was offensive and sarcastic, reprimanding them for either too little or too much zeal, comparing them to their disadvantage with the practitioners of his youth, and rarely missing an oppor-

31

tunity of complaining how standards had fallen.

This dislike of the judge was, however, not restricted to the lawyers. It extended to the local notables, usually retired service officers, who held the post of High Sheriff in the various counties that the Judge of Assize visited on his progress around the circuit. The office of High Sheriff of a county was held for only a year at a time; its duties were mostly ceremonial, supporting the Lord Lieutenant, the King's representative in the county, and involving public appearances at civic functions and raising funds for charities. But the High Sheriff's additional and most important duty was to attend on the visiting judge whom it was his duty to escort to and from his lodgings and the court, sitting not beside him but in the jump seat in the car provided by the local authority, usually an ancient and stately Daimler.

When in court he sat beside the judge, wearing either the uniform of his previous service or formal black court dress with a ceremonial sword. Another obligation was to attend the judge's receptions or dinner parties – which in the case of Mr Justice Plumpton's entertaining was particularly tedious. And unlike the rest of his brethren, Mr Justice Plumpton was known for the high-handed manner in which he treated the High Sheriffs, so that all who had served in that office in the various counties of the West of England that lay within the Western Circuit declared him the most disagreeable, unbearable and pompous little man that they had ever encountered in England, India, Egypt, or wherever in the world their previous duties and stations or ships had taken them. On one famous occasion a retired Captain in the Royal Navy happened to overlook the time and date of the arrival at the railway station of Mr Justice Plumpton, who was coming from London by train to commence the assize, and so was not on the platform to greet him when he descended from his reserved first-class compartment. The High Sheriff was in fact at Salisbury races. Finding no one to receive him, the judge was obliged to get a taxi to take him to the lodgings where he telephoned the Chief Constable and directed him to bring the defaulting High Sheriff to him under arrest. This experience drove the Captain to such an extreme of apoplexy that he retired to his bed, it was said with a case of gin, and pleading illness he refused to rise from his bed until he had heard that Mr Justice Plumpton had moved on into the neighbouring county.

So the dislike of Mr Justice Plumpton was general. It was not known whether he appreciated how universal it was. Some of the bar said that he couldn't, as if he did he would have cut his throat; others said he did but that he gloried in it and that it was up to someone other than the judge himself to cut the judge's throat. Whichever it was, nothing deterred him. The air of the West Country, he said, agreed with him. So when it was learnt in the spring of 1934 that he was coming again for the summer assize, the usual gloom fell upon the bar, the local solicitors and the various High Sheriffs in office that year.

The pleasant summer weeks passed and it was not until towards the end of the circuit that Mr Justice Plumpton reached the county of Dorset. The High Sheriff of Dorset for that year was a certain Colonel Harrington, only recently retired from commanding a district at Quetta near the North-West Frontier of India, and on a sunny day in late July he was sitting beside the judge on the bench at the Dorchester Assizes.

The afternoon was warm; the court airless. There was a lull after a prisoner had been sentenced and taken to the cells down the stairs that led from the dock in the historic eighteenth-century courtroom where a hundred years earlier the so-called Tolpuddle Martyrs – the agricultural workers who had administered secret oaths in the attempt to combine to improve their conditions of labour – had been convicted and sentenced to transportation. The next case had not yet

34

been called and the judge with the Colonel High Sheriff dozing beside him was about to express some judicial witticism at the expense of the counsel who had appeared unsuccessfully for the departing prisoner when a sound like a pistol shot rang round the court. The Colonel opened his eyes. The judge ducked, his head falling well below the level of his desk, his papers scattering on to the floor. It was a time when there had lately been some IRA or Fenian activity, with shots in the streets and bombs exploding in letter-boxes. After a few seconds he re-emerged into sight. Finding that no one was dead and now red-faced with embarrassment that his obvious display of fright had been witnessed by all in the courtroom, he said angrily, 'What was that? Who made that noise?'

He peered down furiously at the row of bewigged counsel sitting on their bench. They in turn looked down at the papers before them. Someone, they knew, was about to get it.

'I did, my lord.'

'Who said that?'

'I did.'

Mr Justice Plumpton bent forward and glared. The speaker was a young man with a very new white wig above a dark, saturnine face seated at the end of the row. 'Stand up when you address me, young man.'

'I can't,' Mordecai Ledbury replied coolly.

The face of the judge reddened. Colonel Harrington, now fully awake, began to anticipate that he might be going to enjoy the afternoon.

'What do you mean, you can't? How dare you speak to me like that? Stand up, I say.'

'I can't,' repeated Mordecai. 'You see, my lord, it was my stick that made such a noise. It fell off the bench and until I retrieve it, I can't get to my feet.'

'You will get to your feet when addressing me, young man, or I shall commit you for contempt.'

'Give me a hand.' Mordecai turned to the barrister sitting next to him. The barrister, an elderly man, put a hand under Mordecai's arm and with an effort Mordecai slowly hauled himself up from his seat until he was leaning forward supporting himself on his two arms with his hands on the bench in front of him. It took time and effort.

'What is this absurd play-acting? Are you jesting with me, sir?' thundered the judge.

'No, my lord, I am not. I need my stick and it has fallen underneath the desk. I suppose you thought it was a gun going off. But that's all it was. Just a stick, nothing worse.'

'Have a care, young man or–'

'I am only trying to explain because–'

'Silence. You have no business coming to my court with a stick and–'

Again Mordecai interrupted him. His

usually pallid face was now as flushed as the judge's. 'Wherever I go I have to have a stick, or rather two sticks. I don't enjoy the same facility as your lordship has in getting about and if I hadn't my sticks I couldn't be here to carry out my duty, which is to plead for the next defendant to appear before your lordship. I am sorry that one of my sticks fell off the desk and made a noise that so rattled you but I cannot think that is a very great crime.'

'I was not rattled and it is impertinent of you to suggest that I was. And I do not care what you think, young man. You have come into my court and created a disturbance. You will leave my court immediately.'

'I can't do that. I have my professional duty to perform. Unless, which I now should welcome, you adjourn my client's case until the next assize for hearing by another judge.'

'I shall do nothing of the kind. How dare you suggest it? You will leave my court and another counsel will take the case.'

'I do not consent to that nor, I am certain, will my client. I am his counsel and I shall remain so. But having regard to your lordship's attitude to my disability, I wish to submit that after this incident it would not now be proper for you to try my client. I apply for an adjournment.'

By now the barristers were awe-struck, the solicitors admiring and the High Sheriff thoroughly amused. Young counsel in the whitest of white wigs was taking on the detestable Mr Justice Plumpton and everyone was enjoying it.

'As I said, young man, you are being impertinent. You come here, lurching into my court with your stick and–'

'I have not lurched into your court. If I sounded to you impertinent, my lord, it was because you appeared to be mocking my disability.'

'I was doing nothing of the kind.' Mr Justice Plumpton managed to sound indignant.

'Well, you've just described me as lurching into your court. You ordered me from your court because one of my sticks, which I need to be able to stand and to walk, unfortunately fell from the desk on to the floor. Because that startled you so much, I apologize. I do not consider that anything I have said is impertinent or has detracted from the respect that I of course owe the bench.'

'Then show some respect and cease arguing with me.'

'I am not arguing with you, my lord, but I do not like being sneered at because I am a cripple. Not even by a judge.'

The judge picked up his gavel and struck wildly on the desk. 'I will have no more of this. Send for the Leader of the Circuit to come to my room. If he is not at Dorchester, send me the senior silk who is. And you, young man, come with him. The court is adjourned.'

The judge got to his feet. The usher shouted, 'All rise,' and Mr Justice Plumpton disappeared through the door behind his chair, followed by his clerk and the High Sheriff.

When they had gone the court broke into a buzz of talk and laughter. The solicitor, an elderly grey-haired man who had been sitting in front of Mordecai, turned to him, smiling. One of the barristers slapped his back. The elderly barrister who had helped him to his feet gathered up his papers and handed him his stick. 'A most promising start to your career on the circuit,' he beamed.

In his room the judge turned to the High Sheriff. 'Did you ever hear such impertinence! I never said anything about his disability. I did not know he had a disability. I've never seen him before in my life.' He turned to his clerk who had joined them. 'Who is that young man?'

'He's a Mr Mordecai Ledbury, who has only recently been elected to the circuit,' the clerk replied.

Mr Justice Plumpton turned back to the High Sheriff. 'Did you hear me say anything about his disability?'

The Colonel smoothed his white moustache. He'd been brusquely received when he had gone to the judge's lodgings that morning and had been treated, he felt, like a servant at the judge's reception on the previous evening – behaviour that he greatly resented.

'You did refer to his – to his lurching into your court, Judge,' he said briskly.

'That was a figure of speech, purely a figure of speech. It was not meant to mock him although it did strike me that he was trying to be impertinent.'

'I suppose he has to lurch if he's so crippled. Unfortunate you mentioned it though.' The Colonel pulled at his white moustache.

The clerk said, 'I'll go and see if the Leader is on his way.' When he left the room, the judge took off his wig and flung himself in a chair. He did not invite the High Sheriff to sit.

'The young man was deliberately and grossly impertinent,' he announced, shaking his head. 'The young whippersnapper.' He stared at the High Sheriff as he went on. 'He was grossly impertinent. It has wasted a whole afternoon of the court's time.'

For five minutes they remained in awkward silence, the Colonel still standing. The clerk returned. 'Mr Cookson QC is here, my lord. He is the senior silk presently in Dorchester. He has been speaking to those who were in court.'

Cookson followed the clerk into the room.

He was a man of about forty, tall, thin and with a grave expression. He shared the general opinion on the circuit about Mr Justice Plumpton. On the previous Monday he had been on the receiving end of the judge's tongue when the latter had commented upon the inadequacy of his cross-examination. Plumpton remembered and felt uneasy.

'Cookson,' he began, 'you have heard what happened in my court earlier this afternoon?'

Cookson bowed slightly. 'I have spoken to some who were present and I understand there has been an altercation with a young counsel,' he said.

'The young man was rude and impertinent in open court.'

'I heard it was a misunderstanding. The young man – he's new on the circuit – has a serious disability. He's a cripple and he's probably rather sensitive about it. He needs his sticks to stand and get about and I gather that it was one of his sticks that started the trouble. When it fell off the bench I hear it sounded like a pistol shot.'

To Mr Justice Plumpton it had sounded exactly like that. Which was why he had ducked – in full view of the court.

The Colonel coughed and Cookson looked at him. 'Perhaps the High Sheriff,' Cookson said, 'has formed an impression about the incident and could help us? As an outside observer, sir, did the young man appear to you to be trying to be impertinent to the judge?'

'A misunderstanding, I thought,' said the Colonel. 'Cross purposes about standing and lurching and sticks. The young fellow, as you say, is probably infernally sensitive. If something like that had happened in the regiment with a senior officer, I'd have thought an apology would have settled it.'

The judge could see how the tide was running. Even the clerk, his own clerk, had been curiously silent.

'Mr Ledbury is here,' said the clerk.

'Show him in.'

The clerk opened the door and, using his two sticks, Mordecai limped slowly into the room. No one spoke and he stopped in the centre of the room.

'If I was rude, Judge, I apologize. If you wish it, I will repeat that apology in open court.'

'I do,' said Plumpton. Mordecai bowed his head in acknowledgment and stumped slowly out.

Five minutes later, with the High Sheriff beside him, Mr Justice Plumpton took his seat in court.

Mordecai got to his feet slowly, using his sticks, and stood with two hands on the desk before him.

42

'Yes, Mr Ledbury,' said the judge.

'If I was rude to the bench earlier this afternoon, I apologize.'

Then with a crash he fell back into his seat. Mr Justice Plumpton was, for once, nonplussed. Somehow he had imagined that the young man would say more, that he would dress up the apology with something more elaborate. But he hadn't. He had said that he would apologize and he had. So there was nothing for him, the judge, but to say as he did, grudgingly, 'Thank you.' He then adjourned for the day. He didn't speak to the High Sheriff during their journey back to the lodgings.

'That young man,' said the Colonel to his wife later that evening when he told her of the incident, 'will go far.'

The Colonel was right. Mordecai had made his name on the circuit. It was felt that Mr Justice Plumpton had been bested and Mr Justice Plumpton thereafter rarely came on the circuit again. At dinner that evening in the hotel where the circuiteers dined, Cookson ordered champagne. Many years later when he was a Lord Justice in the Court of Appeal and Mordecai was famous and Cookson heard reports of Mordecai's difficult behaviour in court towards certain judges, he remembered that afternoon at Dorchester. 'Mordecai's disability,' he drily remarked to one of his brethren, 'has become part of

Mordecai's repertoire. He has made his sticks part of the act. And I was there at the beginning.'

In 1938 Grace Ledbury fell ill with cancer and after many months, some spent in hospital, she died in December 1939, during what came to be called 'the phony war'. Mordecai, by then living in an apartment in the Temple, buried her in the same cemetery at Putney as his father. He made sure however that she lay well away from her husband, her love for whom he had never witnessed.

So Grace was spared the experience of the air raids that began in the autumn of 1940 when every evening Mordecai lay fully dressed on his bed on the top floor of a flimsy eighteenth-century brick house in King's Bench Walk. The building had no lift and he had a horror of being trapped. It was difficult for him to get down the many stairs to the cellar so he lay listening to the sounds and seeing the flashes from the explosion of the bombs. He often thought of his conversation with the dying Aaron. My father was right, he thought. If I die now, I should die ignorant of love.

During the war years and the decade thereafter Mordecai's practice at the bar flourished. Pugnacious, admired by some and disliked by many, he was hugely successful.

He moved from the Temple and took chambers in Albany off Piccadilly. He was now well able to afford the vintage champagne that was his sole alcoholic drink and his holidays in the Cipriani Hotel in Venice. But it was not there that he met the woman who was to provide the one thing that he lacked.

2

Harriet, Countess of Yeovil, was forty-six, tall and graceful and only just past her prime. She had been one of the foremost beauties of the 1930s and '40s. When in 1954, after twenty-five years of marriage, she learnt that Harry, her husband, the Earl, was starting proceedings for divorce she was more hurt than angry.

That he should think of doing such a thing she found deeply wounding. She had done her duty by producing for him a son and heir, Tom, who was now approaching his coming of age, while throughout the marriage she had been uniformly agreeable to her extremely dull husband who lived the year round in a gloomy castle in Northumbria, an existence she naturally couldn't be expected to share. So she spent much of the year in Eaton Square when not on holiday in Paris or Provence. To their separate lives Harry had not, she thought, objected.

She had taken pains to be reasonably discreet in her behaviour with her lovers, who were, she had to admit, a fairly catholic lot.

The first had not been taken, according to convention, until after Tom's birth. He had been the best man at her wedding and a great friend of Harry so she couldn't see why Harry could possibly object to him. The second and third were both during World War II when the Earl was with his Yeomanry regiment in the Middle East. They had, she confessed, been a trifle louche – the first a Polish fighter pilot who was a kleptomaniac and never left her or any other house without a few spoons or a silver snuff-box in his pocket; the second had been the Third Secretary at the Chinese embassy. This last was a momentary affair, which foundered on the first night when, glancing at the bedroom mirror, she caught sight of her lover on top of her and got a fit of giggles. The fourth and latest of her lovers, in post-war Paris, was Henri de Malplaquet, the exquisite follower of Sartre, a scalp that, having regard to Henri's reputation as a lover of his own sex, everyone regarded as a triumph.

The first Harriet knew of Harry's intentions was the service of the petition. She had failed to read the letter before action from her husband's lawyer, perhaps because she had been abroad in the Var with Henri. When she received the petition, or what she described as 'Harry's unkind and appalling notice', she telephoned Harry several times in Northumbria. On each occasion he shouted, 'Fuck off,' and put down the receiver. She reported this to her closest friend, Elizabeth Fanshawe, who told her that she should take the matter seriously and that, as legal papers had been served, she must get herself a lawyer. The family lawyers having been retained by the Earl, another friend said that she ought to try and get a Mr Horace Doubleday, who, the friend said, was the lawyer always hired by theatre people and sharp company promoters.

Doubleday and Co. had offices in Green Street off Piccadilly. Mr Horace Doubleday was very small and bald, sharp, shrewd and astronomically expensive. He invariably dressed in the old-fashioned uniform of his profession, a dark jacket and striped trousers, a starched wing collar and a spotted bow tie. He adopted this conventional guise in the hope that it might conceal from clients his reputation in the profession for exceedingly unconventional practice.

When Harriet was admitted into his opulent room, she gave him one of her dazzling smiles, took his limp hand in her equally limp but gloved one, held it for longer than was usual in such circumstances, and then, uninvited, sank into a chair and lit a cigarette. She handed him the petition and expressed her bewilderment, indeed her resentment, at her husband's unfriendly behaviour. When Mr Doubleday had read the petition, he drew in his breath, wagged his head gravely, pronounced that this was indeed unfriendly and declared that he needed time to consider. He then showed her out. When she had gone he rubbed his little hands delicately together with delight, executed a little jig on the expensive Turkey carpet and congratulated himself on having landed so unexpectedly glamorous a client. A defended, society divorce with many days in court and massive expenses seemed to him providential.

Two days later he telephoned her. He had arranged to take her to a consultation with counsel at four o'clock on the following afternoon at King's Bench Walk in the Temple and he would collect her in a cab at three thirty from her house in Eaton Square.

In the cab, he told her that he had retained a Mr Mordecai Ledbury, a QC in his early forties with a reputation as a redoubtable advocate who, although not a specialist in matrimonial matters, was the most formidable cross-examiner at the bar. He would be guaranteed, Mr Doubleday added with satisfaction, to give the Earl a hot time of it in the witness box. When he said this, Harriet thought of the inarticulate, red-faced Harry and felt sorry for him. Still, she reminded herself, he had brought it on himself.

As they drew up in King's Bench Walk, Mr Doubleday whispered conspiratorially that Mr Ledbury was a cripple so she should not be put out if when they entered his room he failed to rise to greet her. Which was what happened.

The room on the first floor was large, with tall windows and a view across the Inner Temple garden. Mordecai was seated behind a large desk. When Mr Doubleday introduced her, Mordecai waved them into the chairs the clerk had drawn up before retiring and stared steadily at Harriet. She smiled back bravely but she was disconcerted by the large, dark face, the almost bald domed head and the hunched shoulders.

'These allegations,' he began, tapping the petition when she and Mr Doubleday were seated, 'are they true?'

The voice surprised her. It was deep and melodious. It made up somewhat, she thought, for his disagreeable appearance.

'What do you mean?' she replied, still smiling.

'What I said.'

Mr Doubleday squirmed uncomfortably in his chair.

'Is it true,' Mordecai went on, 'that you have committed adultery with the four men whose names are set out in the petition?'

'Adultery.' Harriet shuddered prettily. 'Such an ugly word.' She opened her bag and

49

took out her cigarette case. 'Do you mind?'

Mordecai shook his head, and waited as she lit the cigarette and screwed it into an amber holder.

'In the nineteenth century, it was called crim. con., or criminal connection,' he went on. 'Which is what Lord Melbourne, the Prime Minister, was accused of with Mrs Norton, Sherry's daughter. If that is more delicate and what you prefer, we can call it that. It means the same thing. I repeat. Is the allegation true?'

'Is that important?' She tapped the cigarette on the edge of a small silver tray. He's extraordinarily ugly, she thought.

'It is.'

There was a pause, taken up by more business with the cigarette. Then she said, 'I suppose it could be said to be true.'

'What do you mean by that? Is it true or is it not?'

Harriet sighed. 'If you put it like that, in a way it is.'

'Adultery with four different men?'

'They were certainly all very different.'

'Adultery with four men?'

'But not, I assure you, at the same time.'

Mordecai began to smile, and his smile lit up the whole of his dark face, as if the sun, Harriet thought, had suddenly appeared from behind a bank of cloud. She blew out a circle of smoke. Perhaps he was not so ugly after all.

'So it is four lovers, but one at a time, between 1935 and today, 1954. One after the other. Is that how it was?'

'How it was?' she mused. 'Yes. I suppose that is how it was.' She smiled back at him. Mordecai's smile had disappeared and she wanted to get it back.

'Then there's little we can do for you but–'

Mr Doubleday, appalled, interrupted. This was not what he had planned. 'I am sure,' he said, 'that counsel has considered the fact the onus will be upon the petitioner to prove–'

Mordecai turned on him. 'They would not have launched this petition with its explicit particulars of the four named men, four such diverse co-respondents, unless they had proof.'

Mr Doubleday sank back in his chair. Mr Ledbury might win cases but he for one would not brief Mr Ledbury ever again.

Mordecai turned back to Harriet. 'The four, if I may say so, make such an improbable quartet that it seems to me that your husband must have proof of their guilt and yours.'

'Guilt!' she repeated, stubbing out the half-smoked cigarette. 'You do use disagreeable words about something which, in all the cases except one–' she was thinking of the Chinese Third Secretary – 'was at the time quite delightful.'

She had got her wish, for now Mordecai was smiling again. 'Have you any money, Lady Yeovil?'

'As a matter of fact I have.'

'Then don't waste it on lawyers.'

Mr Doubleday flinched. Mordecai went on.

'Your solicitor here, Mr – Mr...?'

'Doubleday.'

'Mr Doubleday will get you the best deal that he can. You can't defend the petition because what your husband has alleged is true. If you went into court, they would savage you.' He paused, still staring at her.

'Savage me?'

'Of course.'

'Break me,' she murmured, 'like a butterfly on the wheel?' And she laughed.

'Exactly.' Then Mordecai added softly, 'And having met you, I should not like to see that happen.'

Later that evening she telephoned Elizabeth from Eaton Square. 'I've just met a quite extraordinary man. He's a cripple and he's as ugly as sin. He's a lawyer and has an apartment in Albany. I'm going to invite him for dinner.'

'Why?'

'Because he's different.'

'Oh dear,' Elizabeth said. 'Are you off again?'

The dinner party consisted of six. There was Elizabeth, a Hungarian called Lavenchko with a poor command of English but a good appreciation of free food and drink, who remained mostly silent, and Harriet's sister-in-law Bridget, her husband's sister, and Will, her bewildered spouse.

'But why are we going to dine with Harriet?' he had asked. 'Harry is going to divorce her.'

'Never mind that. I like her,' explained Bridget.

In the loo after dinner, Elizabeth said of Mordecai, 'But he's grotesque! He's a monster!'

'I know, darling, I know. Don't stay long, and don't forget to take the Hungarian with you. I'll get rid of the others.'

Unlike her night with the Chinaman, she didn't want to laugh; unlike her affair with Henri, she didn't have to do any coaxing. Unlike the Polish airman here was no braggadocio and unlike Harry's best friend there was a minimum of formality. So the lovemaking with Mordecai she found deeply fulfilling. When she helped him from her bed and watched as he put on his strange boots and thought of him climbing awkwardly into the taxi, she decided that she was deeply grateful that the unreasonable behaviour of the Earl had brought her so unexpected a reward.

Their affair properly began with a few days in Paris, eating and lovemaking at the Crillon, and it continued for five years. Then, on the beach at Portofino, Mordecai suddenly grew bored. In the late autumn and the early winter of that year the love affair slowly but gracefully faded. There were no tears, no recriminations; both expressed themselves devoted to the other.

'Darling,' Harriet said to Elizabeth, 'you must take him on.'

'Oh, no,' Elizabeth replied, 'I couldn't. Not as a lover. But I do rather like him.'

After the break Harriet went away to pass the winter in Rome. When she had gone Mordecai sat alone in his chambers in Albany, drinking his champagne from a tankard, and thought once more of the words his father had pronounced on his deathbed. How true they had been. Men, Aaron had said, are attracted by the eye; women by the ear.

3

Five years after the end of his affair with Harriet, Mordecai heard from Elizabeth that Harriet had been diagnosed with cancer of the ovaries. For two years she fought the disease and during those years Mordecai visited her constantly at Eaton Square and sat with her for hours. Six months before the end, she told him she was going to Northumbria to die in what she had once called 'Harry's gloomy castle', which Tom, her son, had inherited. Sylvia, her daughter-in-law, had asked her to come. They would look after her, Sylvia had said.

'So I'm going,' she told Mordecai. 'It'll be strange ending my days in the place that for years I did my best to avoid. And,' she added, 'I'm running short of cash.'

'If I can help–' Mordecai began.

'Certainly not. This is a family thing and you are not family.'

'No,' he said, 'I'm not.' Neither spoke for a time.

'You know, of course,' she went on, 'that if I had followed the advice of that awful solicitor and had fought the case and not been beguiled by that wicked smile of yours, I might have done better.'

'Why?' he asked.

'Because Tom told me later that at the time Harry was having it off with one of the stable girls – which was why he wanted to get rid of me.'

'But if you'd defended it they still would have been after you for what you had been up to and I didn't want you to be...'

'Broken on the wheel?' She smiled. 'Do you remember?'

'Of course I remember.'

They were silent again for a while. Then he said, 'Harry didn't marry his woman, did he?'

'Not in the end, the wily old brute. After our divorce he got in a panic and paid her off. I think she did better than me financially.'

She was silent for long time. Then she said, 'Do you still see Elizabeth?'

He nodded. 'Often.'

'But she's not one of your women?' She knew that after her there had been other women in Mordecai's life.

'Not in that way. But we're friends. I go and stay at Pemberley.'

'I'm glad. She was a good friend to me.' She stretched out her hand. 'I'm getting tired. Go now, Mordecai. Tom comes tomorrow to take me to the north. I won't see you again.'

He bent forward and kissed her forehead. 'You'll never know' he said, 'how much you meant to me.'

He gathered up his sticks and, without turning back, left the room.

Over the next years he went on seeing Elizabeth. They developed an *amitié amoureuse*, she dining with him in London in his Albany chambers, he visiting Pemberley on the Devonshire-Dorset border.

Elizabeth's husband, Charlie Fanshawe, the Lord Lieutenant of the county, had always got on well with him. Which was unusual. Charlie was a reserved, silent man and he appreciated the often protracted times when all Mordecai wanted was to get away from the other guests and sit in the library and read and smoke. Charlie also enjoyed Mordecai's sudden explosions, often aimed at the outraged guests whom Charlie used to describe as 'Elizabeth's Wah-wahs'. When Elizabeth once asked Charlie why he got on so well with Mordecai, Charlie replied, 'He doesn't suffer fools gladly but he suffers me. That's why I like him.'

It became a tradition for Mordecai to visit over the Whitsun weekend and stay on for the rest of the following week. In 1971, on the Wednesday after Whit Sunday, Elizabeth said to him, 'You have to pay a price. Charlie has told me he can't come to a dinner on Thursday. He has some official engagement so you'll have to escort me.'

She didn't tell him what the occasion was because she suspected that if he knew he'd refuse and leave for London. For the dinner at which she needed an escort was a dinner party at the judge's lodging at Exminster given by an old school friend of Charlie's, Edmund Wetherby, the judge who would be presiding at the Exminster Assize. 'Please, you must go,' Charlie had said to Elizabeth when he told her he would not be able to come, 'I promised Edmund that you would.

Take Mordecai. He'll enjoy it.'

Elizabeth knew that Mordecai would not enjoy it. So she didn't tell him where they were going until they met in the library in their evening clothes. Charlie's school friend, Edmund Wetherby, was admired and liked in the profession because he was a sound lawyer, a good judge and courteous and polite to everyone who had business in his court – even to the accused whom he had to try and frequently to sentence.

He liked to go on the Western Circuit because his home was within its boundaries and he could easily get back each weekend, and he was always pleased when he was the senior judge, for then he could look forward to entertaining his many friends to dinner in the lodgings, an attractive Regency house within the Cathedral close. The only other judge to be with him on this assize was a new judge, Helena Fulbright, and the Lord Chief Justice had sent her out with Edmund Wetherby as being the best person to introduce her to the life of a Judge of Assize.

Helena was fifty-five years of age but looked older. Of her the bar declared that she was less of an old woman than many of her colleagues on the High Court bench. Edmund Wetherby flattered himself that he could persuade her to fit in with his plans for entertaining and that even if she would be no ornament at his dinner parties she would not object to his programme. He decided that his first entertainment would have to be for an official group, a small party for the Lord Mayor, to which he had begged his old friend – Charlie Fanshawe, the Lord Lieutenant, to come and help him out.

On the Friday, the last working day of their first week in Exminster, he was sitting beside Helena Fulbright, both in their robes, as they were conveyed in the stately municipal Daimler from the lodgings to the Castle where he was trying the criminal list and she the civil. In the jump seat in front of them sat the High Sheriff dressed in the dark frock coat and black forage cap of his former regiment in the Foot Guards.

Edmund Wetherby leant forward. 'George,' he enquired, 'have you heard from the Lord Mayor and the others whether they can dine next week?'

'Yes, Judge, they're all on. The Lord Mayor and Chief Constable and their wives are delighted to accept, but there was a call from the Lord Lieutenant. He's going to give a ring today at lunchtime. I fear something may have come up.'

At the luncheon adjournment the High Sheriff had the answer. 'The Lord Lieutenant is very sorry but he has to call it off. Royalty is visiting the town but Lady Fanshawe would be delighted to come. He said they have a house guest, a man, and may she

59

bring him?'

'Tell her, of course.'

It was only on the Tuesday morning before the dinner on the Thursday that the High Sheriff told the judge, 'Lady Fanshawe's escort is someone she says you'll know. Mordecai Ledbury.'

'Good God! Mordecai!' Edmund flung himself back in his seat. He turned to Mrs Justice Fulbright. 'Have you come across him?'

'Not personally,' she said grimly. 'I've heard he can be rather controversial.'

'He certainly can! Damn Elizabeth! Depending on Mordecai's mood, he can make or mar a dinner party. But it's too late do anything about it now.'

At eight o'clock on Thursday Mordecai Ledbury, in a bad temper and a dinner jacket with an old-fashioned high stiff wing collar, limped after Elizabeth Fanshawe as he followed her into the lodgings. He was as reluctant to be there as his host was to receive him. When Elizabeth had told him in the library where they were going he said he'd be damned if he'd come; he'd catch the night train back to London.

'Oh, no you won't. You're coming to Edmund's party with me.'

'Why should I? I've come down here to get away from the law. A pompous judges' dinner party with a lot of local bores! No, I'll go home to London.'

'You'll do nothing of the kind. You are going to take me. You are our guest at Pemberley and Edmund is one of Charlie's oldest friends. I've already told him you are escorting me. And mind you behave.'

At the entrance to the drawing room, Edmund Wetherby greeted Elizabeth with a kiss, gave Mordecai a friendly pat on the back and introduced them to the rest of the party who had arrived before them. There were six, the High Sheriff and his wife, the Chief Constable and his wife, and the Lord Mayor of Exminster with the Mayoress.

They were, thus, a party of ten seated at the round table in the dining room. Edmund was flanked by Elizabeth and the Lady Mayoress; Helena Fulbright by the Lord Mayor and the Chief Constable. Mordecai was seated between the Lady Mayoress and the Chief Constable's wife. The former was jolly, with a large bosom and a double chin; the latter, craggy and aggressive. The husband of the latter had only recently been appointed to his new post, coming from being Deputy Chief Constable in the Home Counties, and she was determined to show that she was quite as good as any of the other dignitaries assembled in the judge's drawing room. At first the jolly Mayoress chatted away to Mordecai who had to do little but nod and now and then put a disinterested question. But when Edmund turned to the Mayoress and the Chief Constable's wife turned to a silent Mordecai, she began by asking if Mordecai lived locally or was visiting.

'Visiting,' he replied laconically.

The Chief Constable's wife paused, then she said, 'My name's Lily Turner. What's yours and what do you do?'

For answer Mordecai pushed the place card with his name on it towards her. Mr Mordecai Ledbury QC. She peered at it. 'Oh,' she said, 'a barrister. My husband,' she went on, inclining her head towards where her husband sat next to Helena, 'is the Chief Constable.'

Mordecai nodded. He had refused Edmund's excellent claret and asked for more of the champagne they had been drinking before dinner. He now took a substantial swallow. Lily began a lecture, about the burden on the modern police officer and of the long, weary hours they put in, especially her husband. When there was no response from Mordecai, she brought up the subject of the bar and said how objectionable the police found many barristers who so often treated police officers to unfair cross-examination. Mordecai remained silent but Lily went on, saying the police greatly resented this behaviour by the bar.

For the first time Mordecai turned to look

at her. 'Why should they be resentful?' he asked.

'Why?' she repeated. 'Because it's most unfair.'

'It's often deserved,' Mordecai growled.

Lily bent her head towards him. 'I'm sorry. I didn't catch what you said.'

'I said,' Mordecai repeated more loudly, 'that they often deserved it.'

The Chief Constable's wife drew herself up in her chair and glared at him. 'How can you say that? Police officers are only doing their duty.'

'So is counsel.'

'But they are paid.'

'So are the police.'

Two patches of scarlet now glowed on the cheekbones of the Chief Constable's wife. 'But there is no need for the lawyers to attack police officers so offensively,' she said.

'Counsel attacks them when they deserve it. Too often nowadays they are corrupt.'

She began to bridle. 'How can you say such a thing?'

'I say it because it's true. The Flying Squad in the Metropolitan Police in London is notoriously riddled with corruption.'

'I am sure that is not so. Anyway, my husband commands a provincial force–'

'Which itself, I expect, contains a due proportion of rogues.'

During this last exchange there had been a

pause in the general conversation around the dinner table. The Chief Constable, two places away, like the others had overheard it and began to glower.

'What are you on about, Mordecai? Are you on one of your high horses?' Edmund Wetherby said pleasantly.

'If you mean that my low opinion of the present police service is one of my high horses, then I am.'

'And what is your opinion, Mr Ledbury, of the police service?' said the Chief Constable ominously, leaning forward.

'From what he has just said,' the Lady Mayoress broke in with a loud laugh, 'I gather it's not very high.'

'No,' said Mordecai, 'it is not.' Elizabeth stared at him across the table. Shut up, she mouthed silently. But Mordecai would not. 'There have been too many cases recently of police corruption. Ever since the war and the black market with criminal money washing around in the underworld, the police have got too close to the criminals. It's unhealthy. In London corruption in the Met is rife. I've no doubt that it is general right across every police force in the country.'

'I hope you are not including this county,' said the Chief Constable, leaning across the table.

'If the shoe fits,' Mordecai said.

'Come, come, Mordecai,' Edmund intervened. He turned to the others. 'Mordecai doesn't come down here often enough for him to judge. He's too busy earning vast fees in the libel court and the appeal courts in London. The judges, I can assure you, Chief Constable, have complete confidence in the local constabulary.'

'I've said what I have to say,' Mordecai growled.

Edmund looked pointedly at Helena Fulbright and nodded.

'I think we might have coffee in the drawing room?' Helena said and pushed back her chair. She turned to Elizabeth. 'Perhaps, Lady Fanshawe, we should retire.'

As the men sat round their port and Mordecai drank champagne, the others ignored him. The High Sheriff started to talk about the improvement in the number of partridges locally and how a mild summer might postpone the pheasants until well into December.

In the car on the way home, Elizabeth said, 'Whatever made you be so offensive?'

'The wife,' Mordecai replied, huddled back in the corner of the Bentley, 'was deliberately provocative.'

'You shouldn't have reacted. You were very wrong, and you know it. You've made an enemy tonight in her husband.'

'That doesn't worry me. I won't come across him again.'

'For your sake, I hope you don't.'

In the police car the Chief Constable was still raging. 'Arrogant brute! If ever I get my hands on that fellow, I'll teach him a lesson.'

In the lodgings as Edmund turned off the lights in the drawing room, he said to Helena, 'That was Mordecai all over. He can't resist getting into a quarrel. I told you he could make or mar a dinner party. Well, tonight, he certainly marred ours. Confound the fellow.'

Chapter Three

1

Thomas, clerk to Mordecai Ledbury QC, directed the taxi through the Lord Chancellor's entrance, then left along the passage that divided the north from the south part of the House of Lords. He told the driver to wait and slipped up the stairs past the robing room into the Central Lobby. Then he mounted more stairs and went along the corridor to the room where the Judicial Committee of the House of Lords was in session.

He entered and found a chair along the wall behind counsel's seats, facing the five Law Lords who were sitting at their

66

horseshoe table under a great tapestry hanging on the wall above them. While the barristers were in wigs and gowns, the five judges of the House of Lords were without any robes and in plain clothes, for although this was the final Court of Appeal for the United Kingdom, it was constitutionally a Committee of the Legislature. So these judges, the Law Lords, wore the plain dress of peers ordinarily attending the House.

In the centre of the five, and presiding, was Mackintosh Renfrew, a Scottish lawyer, one-time Lord Advocate and a rugged, fresh-faced man originally from Aberdeen. Although now well into his seventies he was as alert and shrewd as ever, the most distinguished judge of his generation – and the only judge in the world for whom Mordecai Ledbury had unqualified and ungrudging respect.

It was almost four o'clock on a Thursday afternoon, shortly before the court, or rather the Committee, would adjourn, and as Thomas took his place he could see the back of his principal, Mordecai Ledbury, standing, in fact leaning against the lectern that was positioned between counsel's desks and from which they addressed the Law Lords. He had the crooks of his two sticks hooked on to the edge of the lectern. His gown was well off his shoulders, half-way down the hump of his back, and his wig was as usual askew, slanted across his immense, dark face.

'Have ye anything further ye wish to add, Mr Ledbury?' asked Lord Renfrew, looking up at the clock. It was the final day of the four during which the Law Lords had been hearing a complicated patent appeal between two multinational pharmaceutical corporations.

'No, my lord. I have wearied your lordship for long enough with my submissions–'

He was interrupted by the wingman on the horseshoe table, the Law Lord sitting on Renfrew's far right, a dapper, sour-looking individual with sleeked-back hair and horn-rimmed spectacles. 'Have you nothing...' He paused before adding, '...nothing at all further to submit on the case of Lester and the Welcome Trust?'

Mordecai turned his great head and shifted his glance from Renfrew to the questioner, the most junior of the five judges. This was Lord Marriott, for whom Mordecai had no time, not when Marriott had been at the bar and especially not since when, as Mordecai put it, 'Marriott had creeped his way up the judicial ladder.' He shook his head slowly. 'I have not,' he said shortly.

'Nothing at all?'

'Nothing.' Mordecai spoke sharply. 'As I indicated to my lord, I have completed my submissions.'

Lord Renfrew smiled. Like Mordecai he too did not have much time for this particular colleague. 'Very well,' Renfrew said, 'then we are finished with argument.'

He nodded to the senior attendant, an immensely tall man in tailcoat and white tie, with a medallion on a gold chain on his breast. 'Clear the bar,' the attendant called.

Mordecai took his sticks, bowed to Lord Renfrew and, leaving Thomas to collect his papers, made for the door. The other counsel gathered up their briefs and started to leave. They were followed by the solicitors for the parties, the executives of each of the pharmaceutical companies, and the few members of the public who had been interested in the case and who had been seated by the wall at the back of the room. It took a little time for the bar to clear, for Mordecai moved slowly. Lord Marriott, watching him, shook his head and gave an audible sigh cut short by the look he received from Mackintosh Renfrew. Mordecai with his hands on his two sticks waited by the door for someone to open it for him and then headed the procession out into the corridor. The room emptied except for the Law Lords, left to their deliberations and still seated at their table.

Outside the Committee room, Mordecai, crab-like on his sticks, moved slowly down the corridor to the lift, overtaken by the other counsel and occupants of the Committee room. Charley Whitby, his junior counsel, joined him.

'Well?' said Charley. 'What do you think?'

'If they are three to two against us,' growled Mordecai, 'the swing vote in the five will be that of that ass Marriott. But we have Mackintosh. That's all that matters.'

'Not for the client, not if they are three to two against us.'

'No, but Mackintosh knows we are right. That's enough for me.'

It may be for you, thought Whitby as they entered the lift, but you won't be paying the costs or the damages. In the lift Mordecai saw the troubled look on his junior's face. 'In fact,' he growled, 'I think they're four to one for us – the one against us will, of course, be Marriott.'

In the robing room on the ground floor, Thomas helped Mordecai off with his robes, handed him a clean shirt and packed the robes into a suitcase. 'Is the taxi here?' Mordecai asked, putting his links into the shirt.

'It is, Mr Ledbury.'

'You'll have to get another to take you back to chambers. I'm going straight home.'

'But the young solicitor from Dorset is coming to see you. I told you this morning. A private matter, he said it was.'

'Tell him I've gone home. If he considers it sufficiently important, send him to Albany in an hour. Not before.'

Mordecai had emerged from the shower and was in his dressing gown, an extravagant red silk garment with a dragon emblazoned in gold on the back, the gift – on top of the immense fee – from a grateful Hong Kong client after Mordecai's efforts in 1970 over the intricacies of land law and what were known as Certificate Bs had turned the millionaire into a billionaire. He was opening a bottle of Bollinger non-vintage champagne for his regular evening drink when the bell of his ground-floor apartment rang. He went to the door and opened it.

'Mr Ledbury?'

'Yes.' It was a youngish man in his late thirties with a ruddy, countrified complexion, dressed in a tweed suit and carrying a briefcase. 'What do you want?'

'My name is Henry Stapleton. I'm a partner in Prescott and Sons of Stoneleigh in Dorset. This is not a professional call, Mr Ledbury. It's a private matter.'

'What do you mean by a private matter?'

'May I come in and explain?'

For answer Mordecai turned and limped back into the drawing room, calling over his shoulder, 'Shut the door behind you.'

He stood beside the table on which he had put the open bottle in its cooler. Stapleton began: 'I am the executor of the will of a gentleman who died last week.'

71

'Well?'

'He was a Major Roderick Fairbairn, the son of your uncle, General Maurice Fairbairn, who was the brother of Grace Ledbury, your mother.'

'The Fairbairns! My mother's family? I've never had anything to do with them and I've never wanted to. Nor have they with me. My father told me that my mother always refused to have anything to do with them. So I didn't either. I've never heard of a Major Fairbairn.'

Stapleton began to undo the latch of his briefcase. 'I have some papers here. May I sit down?'

Mordecai pointed to a chair, shifting the wine cooler to one side. He remained standing.

'Roderick Fairbairn was a hero in World War II during which he was decorated and very badly wounded. He was captured in the desert, lost an eye and an arm and was terribly disfigured. He was repatriated in 1944 before the end of the war. Once home he refused treatment for his scarring and for twenty-seven years lived alone, a recluse, a hermit, seeing nobody. My uncle, Henry Prescott, was the Fairbairns' family solicitor. He knew Major Roderick Fairbairn's father, the General, and before my uncle died twenty years ago used now and then to visit Major Fairbairn. He was the only person

Roderick Fairbairn would let into the house. Our firm has always handled the family's affairs and I took over after my uncle's death. But there was very little that I had to do. Major Fairbairn gave us power of attorney and we received all his income, which was considerable, his father the General having left a tidy sum when he died in 1940. Today that sum has increased very considerably but all we had to do was to send monthly a small amount in cash to Kingsford Langley post office where Major Fairbairn collected it and used it to buy his provisions. It was a very modest sum but he said that was all that he needed. With regard to the family house where he lived, we paid all the household bills, electricity and rates and taxes and so on direct.'

'You said the family house?'

'Yes, it's been in the family for generations. It's called Water Meadow House and is near to the hamlet of Kingsford Langley, which is five miles from Stoneleigh where we have our office. I only saw Major Fairbairn once – when he was alive, that is.'

'When he was alive?'

'Yes, the next time I saw him he was dead. All these years since 1944 he lived there alone in that house as I said, like a hermit. My uncle told me that after he'd been repatriated and was about to start treatment for his burnt and scarred face at the hospital in East Grinstead that specialized in such cases, he learnt that the girl who he was to have married was killed in an air raid – in fact when what they called a buzz-bomb, a flying bomb or V1 landed on the Guards Chapel during Divine Service in June 1944. When he heard this, Major Fairbairn left the hospital and came home. Thereafter he never left the house except to collect his money and provisions. No one came to see him; even the postman stopped coming because there was never any mail. The place, I may add, is in a pretty shocking condition.' He took out a red bandanna handkerchief and mopped his brow.

'I think,' Mordecai said abruptly, 'you'd better join me in a drink.'

He turned on his heel and disappeared. Stapleton laid some papers on the table and waited. Mordecai returned with two glasses. Stapleton looked doubtfully at the bottle and the tall flute glasses. He would have preferred beer or whisky.

'There's nothing else,' Mordecai said, 'unless you want water.'

He poured the champagne, pushed a glass towards Stapleton and collapsed into a chair, flinging his stick down beside it. 'What you have to say is very interesting but what has it to do with me?'

'Two months ago I received a letter at the office from him, informing me that he wanted to see me, to make his will, that it would be very straightforward and that I was to come to Water Meadow House that Friday. As the message referred to a will I brought two assistants as witnesses and a simple form for a will.'

Stapleton paused before he went on. 'It was very eerie. The house was so dilapidated that it looked as if it was about to fall down. The grounds were completely overgrown. Major Fairbairn met us at the front door. He was tall, but very bent, with a beard and long white hair, looking much older than his age which must have been less than sixty. His face was horribly disfigured, with a great scar up the left side from the chin to the brow. And of course, a black patch over one eye.' Stapleton took a sip of wine, then another. 'He took us to the kitchen where I prepared the will which he signed and my assistants witnessed it.'

'You said that when you saw him for the second time he was dead?'

'Yes, I found his body. The postmistress was worried because for some time he hadn't come to collect his money and she thought he might be ill so she telephoned me and I went along to the house. It must have been about a month after I'd been there for his will. This, by the way, was very straightforward – at least it was in regard to the bulk of his fortune. He left this to the

Queen Victoria Hospital in East Grinstead where Sir Archibald McIndoe used to treat those badly burnt in the war, especially the pilots. It was from this hospital that Major Fairbairn had fled after his fiancée's death. With regard to Water Meadow House, it was not so simple. It was my task to locate the person to whom he had bequeathed it, and not only the house and its grounds but also all its contents and the family papers. He had bequeathed this to any surviving child of his father's sister. If none existed, the house was to be sold and the money added to the residue.'

Stapleton paused. 'I've ascertained that the only child was you.'

Mordecai drank and pointed at the bottle. Stapleton stretched across the table and filled Mordecai's glass and his own.

'You are correct,' said Mordecai. 'Grace Fairbairn married Aaron Ledbury. They had only one child and that was me.' He paused, looking down at his feet in their medical boots. 'My mother was a difficult and un-happy woman,' he said, almost to himself. He looked up at Stapleton and asked sharply, 'How did Fairbairn die?'

'The autopsy said it was from a massive heart attack, which was followed by a fall which had broken his neck. I found him lying at the bottom of the stairs so he must have had the attack when he was on the landing at the top of the stairs and fallen the whole length of the staircase. His head was broken open and covered in congealed blood. It was a ghastly sight.'

'Who let you into the house when you found him?'

'The front door was open. At least it was ajar. He must have been lying there for several days.' Stapleton drank again.

'Why should the door be open?'

'I don't know. The police think he may have been about to go down the stairs to shut it when he had the attack and fell. One of the banisters is loose. The whole place, as I say, is in an appalling condition. It can't have been touched for thirty years. In most of the rooms there are sheets over the furniture covered in inches of dust; some of the doors are almost off their hinges, some of the windows are broken. One in the dining room I had boarded up as it's on the ground floor. They told me in the village that Major Fairbairn was only ever seen when he came to collect his money from the post office but local kids sometimes went into the grounds. Before he chased them away they used to hear him talking to himself as he walked or when he sat, as he often did, on a bench overlooking the river. The house is by a river. That's why it is called Water Meadow House.'

'Did no one ever go to the house?'

'No one in the village had been there since World War II. Having been through the place with the police when I found him, I think he only lived in three rooms, the bedroom at the top of the stairs, the kitchen and the library. There are books and papers everywhere in the library.'

'What kind of papers?'

'All kinds. On the table near what must have been his chair by the fire was a whole pile of letters. I never touched them. Some were very old, yellow and crumpled. When we witnessed his will he was very emphatic that none of the papers were to be touched except by the person who inherited the house.'

There was a long silence. Then Stapleton said, 'You can, of course, reject the bequest if you wish.'

'I know that,' growled Mordecai.

Stapleton coloured. 'Of course. It will have to be valued for death duties,' he added.

'It doesn't sound a very agreeable place in which to live. And I dislike the country.' Again there was another long silence. Mordecai passed a hand over his face. 'But I'm interested in the papers and the letters. They could be bundled up and sent here, I suppose?'

'They could, but there are great piles of them. There are literally trunks full of them and there are papers even stuck between the books on the shelves. Someone would have to go through them.'

There was a pause. Then Mordecai said, 'You, of course, have the key to the house?'

'Yes.'

'So if I came down you could meet me and let me in?'

'Yes, certainly.'

There was another pause. 'Is there electricity?'

'Yes, although it's a bit uncertain. I imagine the wiring is very old. There's no telephone now. Major Fairbairn had it disconnected in, I believe, 1944 when he first came home.'

'Water, plumbing?'

'I think so. It would take many hours to go through the papers.'

'So I imagine.' Mordecai sat for a long time in silence. He was thinking of Grace. This house had been her childhood home. Why had she left it? Why had she never wished to see any of her family again? What had they done to her or what had she done to them to estrange them so? Might the letters or papers give him some clue and perhaps explain the nature of the woman who had so rarely been kind to him when he was a child?

'I shall come down,' he said at last, 'and take a look. As you say there are so many papers, I might even pass a night there.'

Stapleton looked doubtful. 'Spend a night in the house?'

'Why not? It would give me more time to look through them. I suppose the stove works and I'll make my own arrangements about food. You could meet me there?'

'I could, but it would be very uncomfortable to stay there.'

'Maybe, but I should like to see it and I should like to look through the papers.'

'If that is what you wish, you have only to let me know when you will be coming.'

'Very well, expect to hear from me.' Mordecai looked out the window at the fading evening light. 'Thank you for coming,' he said, 'and now you'd better be off. Leave your card. I'll telephone to tell you when I can be down. It will be in August when the courts rise. Show yourself out. I can't get up. Too difficult.'

Stapleton put his card on the table, returned the papers to his briefcase, snapped it shut and went to the door. Then he stopped and turned. 'I don't know if it's quite my place to say this, Mr Ledbury, but before I knew you were the heir, I'd heard your name mentioned locally.'

Mordecai looked at him, surprised. 'My name mentioned in Stoneleigh?'

'One of my partners was talking to the local Superintendent of police. Just previously there'd been a conference of senior officers with the Chief Constable and the treatment the police sometimes received at the hands of counsel in the courts came up. The police were complaining about the conduct of certain barristers.'

'What about?'

'That the bar treated them unfairly when cross-examining them, suggesting they are liars and as crooked as the villains that were being tried and so on. As a result, they said, many of the villains they had arrested after grave difficulty got wrongfully acquitted and were set free to rob and terrorize the public even more than before.'

'The police often say that,' Mordecai growled. 'Counsel have a job to do. They often have to question police conduct – and quite rightly.'

'Of course, but apparently our local police seem to be particularly fed up at present. I only mention it because the Superintendent said their Chief used your name as the kind of barrister who was violently anti-police. He said you'd once blackguarded them in his presence.'

'Perhaps I did. There are too many corrupt police today.'

'The local Superintendent told my partner that the Chief Constable was very strong about it. As I said, this was before I knew your connection to Roderick Fairbairn.'

'Tittle-tattle,' Mordecai growled. 'Why are you bringing this up now?'

'I just thought I ought to mention it.'

Stapleton grinned. 'Just in case you come down to Water Meadow House, and get caught speeding.'

'I don't drive,' Mordecai said pouring himself another glass. 'I can look after myself.'

'I'm sure you can. I'll expect to hear from you, then.'

After Stapleton had gone, Mordecai sat thinking about his mother and his boyhood. Why had she left home before her marriage to Aaron? Why had she never wished to see any of her family again? What was the quarrel and why had there been such a feud in the family? As a boy he'd often wondered why she'd never spoken of her own childhood or of her home or of her family. He hadn't even known that she had a brother, the uncle who was apparently the General Stapleton had spoken about. Why when times had been so hard for her, when Aaron was having one of his periods 'resting' and money was so short, had she never turned to them? It was as though for her they did not exist. And now, he thought, I, her son, am the heir to the house where she was brought up. That would have amused his father. Aaron would have enjoyed the irony of that.

Mordecai smiled and poured himself more wine as he thought of the father he had so adored.

He wouldn't want the house, of course. But he'd like to take a look at it, the home of his ancestors. Above all he'd like to take a look at the papers. So, yes, he would go down. He would see what if anything his inheritance might reveal.

2

They had started later than planned and the drive had taken longer than expected. There was heavy traffic on their way out of London and as it was a Saturday morning in August they were further held up by the procession of cars and holiday caravans, especially at Stonehenge.

Mordecai sat in the back of the hired limousine behind his regular driver. On the seat beside him was work, a bundle of papers tied with pink tape, the preliminary instructions in a proposed libel action about which he was to have a consultation on the following Tuesday even though it was the Long Vacation. The client was a young actress of whom Mordecai had never heard but about whose behaviour a gossip columnist had written a cheeky paragraph to which she had taken hysterical offence. She had insisted on having a consultation with counsel about 'her rights', as she had put it.

By the time they had reached the turn-off to Wincanton Mordecai had gone through the bundle. Silly child, he thought, as he tossed the last page aside. She'd be even sillier were she to take the matter to court and he would tell her so. Presumably she was pretty so he'd look forward to seeing her. He would be at his most avuncular, with the charm he reserved for all pretty women but did not bother to waste on men, who had to put up with the abrupt and peremptory manner that he used in court.

He busied himself in gathering the papers together and tying them with the pink tape; then he looked out of the window to watch the hedge-lined fields of Somerset flying past – at a better pace than had the Surrey and Hampshire countryside earlier in the journey. Not that he appreciated the countryside; he preferred the streets and squares of the metropolis for he had a Johnsonian love of London. There was only one reason that he was making this journey from the city – curiosity.

That the house they were going to was the ancestral home of his mother's family meant little to him. If it had come from his father's family and provided some link to Aaron's past or lifted some veil from the mystery of Aaron's origins, he would have turned the house into a shrine. As it was, he'd sell it. He had no interest in anything Fairbairn – as he had no affection for Grace. He had no reason for any. But he did have curiosity, and as the days had passed since Stapleton told him of the bequest, the curiosity had become all-consuming. He was indeed surprised to discover how interested he was to know more about the woman that Aaron had married, the woman who had borne him and who had never loved him. He knew from his father that his arrival in the world had ruined Grace's marriage for her, had brought to an end the few months of what had been for her such perfect bliss. His birth had been the catalyst. He understood from what Aaron had told him that it had ended the sexual passion that she had conceived for Aaron when first they had married. After his birth, that passion had withered and died.

But what had been her life before she was married? He knew from what his father had told him that she had been an art student and that when the two had met she was living the bohemian life, passionate about her painting. But why had she rejected so completely her childhood and her life with her family at Kingsford Langley? What had led her to cut herself off so finally and utterly from her family that even when times had been hard and she was so unhappy she never turned to them? It was the hope of finding an answer to this question that had brought him on this trip.

'Where are we, Webster?' he asked suddenly. 'It's getting late.'

'I know, sir, but we turn south now and we

should be in Dorchester in half an hour. From the map it should be less than an hour from here.'

Stapleton had sent instructions, and drawn a small sketch of the last mile or so of the journey.

'I said I'd be there at lunchtime.'

'We'll be there at two.' After a pause, Webster chuckled. 'In time for a late lunch from that hamper of yours. And a good drink from all those bottles we've brought.'

Webster, like Thomas, Mordecai's clerk, was a favourite, one of the few privileged enough to tease him. Webster was also the owner of the hire company Mordecai used and Mordecai always insisted that Webster should drive him whenever he needed a car.

'Those bottles have to last me through lunch and what could be a long evening – as well as breakfast tomorrow,' he said.

'You're definitely going to spend the night there?'

'I am.'

'Well, I hope the wine will stay cool enough for you, sir.'

'It should.' As well as the hamper they had brought a wine cooler or leather carrier in which was packed ice to surround the three bottles of champagne.

'Where are you spending the night?' Mordecai asked.

'In Stoneleigh, a small town about five

miles away. There's a pub there that takes commercials. There's nothing in Kingsford Langley. At least, there is a pub, but not one for staying.'

'You mean it's not grand enough for you.'

'That's about it, sir.'

'Well, there's no telephone at the house so I can't get in touch with you. Just be back at ten in the morning without fail. I want to be back in London in the early afternoon.'

At two o'clock precisely they stopped at a broken-down gate swinging on its hinges. Beyond them was a derelict cottage, which had once been the lodge.

'This is it, sir,' said Webster as he got out to push back the gate. Mordecai laboriously transferred himself to the front seat beside Webster so that he could the better see as they drove through the grounds.

'Gloomy old place,' Webster said, looking at the tangled, overgrown undergrowth. 'And the drive is nothing but potholes and ruts. It'll play the devil with my springs.'

Mordecai grunted, thinking of what the place must have looked like in its heyday when Grace was a little girl. Grace playing around the place with her brother, the man who had become a general. Then he remembered how much older the brother had been. No, it must have been a lonely childhood. He peered at the dark rhododendron bushes with their great twisted roots and their

87

branches that in places almost formed an arch over the drive, while Webster cursed under his breath, more anxious than ever for the axles of his precious limousine as he slowly manoeuvred around the potholes. 'Rum,' Webster kept repeating. 'A rum old place.'

Sinister, thought Mordecai, for although it was a fine August day little of the sunshine penetrated the overhanging trees and shrubs.

At last they came slowly round a bend and saw before them the house – low and dark with creeper over its walls and shutters over most of the windows. A small car was parked before the front door. Webster drew up beside it and hastened to the passenger door to help Mordecai out. Henry Stapleton came from the front door.

'You found the place all right?' he called.

Mordecai nodded, balancing himself on his two sticks as he looked around him. The frames of the windows had lost most of their paint; the shutters were battered, a lead drainpipe hung loose from one gutter. Again he tried to imagine it in its prime with the young child in a white dress running to the door in the days of Queen Victoria.

'Are you really sure you want to spend the night here? You know you could stay in Stoneleigh. You'd be far more comfortable there.'

Mordecai shook his head and moved slowly towards the front door. He was going to spend at least one night under the roof of his mother's home. 'I'm sorry we're late. Show me the inside.'

'Well, you're not going to be very comfortable but as you sounded so determined on the telephone I brought some sheets and made up a bed for you. I've also lit the stove for hot water.'

'You've done very well. Thank you.'

'Have you brought provisions?' Henry went on.

'I have.'

By now they were in the dark hall, with the shafts of sunlight coming from the open door. Webster came behind them with the hamper and the carrier with the wine.

'Where shall I put these?' he asked.

Henry led him through the hall and dining room to a kitchen. Little daylight penetrated the creeper over the windows and the closed shutters and as they went he had to switch on the lights.

'Spooky old place,' Webster said as he dumped the hamper and the wine carrier on the kitchen table and looked around him. 'The guv'nor shouldn't be spending the night here.' He shook his head disapprovingly

'I know,' Henry replied. 'But he's made his mind up. Nothing we say will stop him.'

Mordecai had remained in the hall, the

sunlight behind him, looking up through the gloom to the staircase and the landing from where presumably Roderick Fairbairn had fallen to his death. The other two returned from the kitchen. 'Is this where you found him?' Mordecai asked, pointing with a stick to the floor below the bottom stair.

Henry nodded. 'It was a nasty sight. He'd been there for some days. The blood had dried black. The door was open so the foxes might have–' He broke off, then went on quietly, 'But they hadn't touched him.'

'Shall I take this upstairs?' Webster asked, putting the dressing case on the floor.

'I'll take it,' said Henry.

'Then I'll be off, sir,' Webster went on more cheerfully. He'd be glad to be away. The place smelt of damp and rot.

'Don't spend all night in the bar. Remember, you must be back here at ten.'

Henry closed the front door behind Webster, shutting out the sunshine. He turned on the hall light and they heard the limousine move off down the drive.

'Where would you like to start? Upstairs?'

Mordecai nodded. 'But it'll take a time for me to get up them.'

Picking up the dressing case, Henry stood beside him, step by step, as Mordecai mounted the stairs, one hand on the banister, his sticks in the other. 'Careful now,' Henry said when they came to where

90

one post stood loose.

On the landing Henry opened the door facing the top of the stairs. 'It's the main bedroom,' he said and pressed the light switch, which turned on a bedside lamp. 'I've made up a bed for you here.' He pointed to the four-poster.

Mordecai remained in the doorway, looking around him. 'Open the window,' he said. Henry put the dressing case on the bed and flung open the window. The sunshine poured into the room. Mordecai went to the chest on which stood a photograph in the silver frame. 'Who is that?'

'It must be the girl Major Fairbairn was to have married and who was killed in an air raid.'

Mordecai picked up the photograph and examined it lengthily before replacing it. She was beautiful.

'The bathroom is along the corridor,' said Henry.

They went down the corridor, Henry turning on the lights, opening the doors of each room. The furniture was covered in sheets, grey with dust, cobwebs swinging in the draught from the ill-fitting windows. 'There's a back staircase that leads to another floor above.'

Presumably where the nursery would have been, where Grace must have lived, Mordecai thought. But he shook his head. 'Too much effort. The papers,' he said, 'that's what I've come for. Show me the papers.'

When they came downstairs to the library, they stood in the doorway and Henry pressed the switch by the door. A single lamp on the small table was the only light. Except for an armchair on the far side of the fireplace with a table beside it, the floor was almost wholly covered by cardboard boxes.

'What are these?' Mordecai asked.

'Boxes of papers, family documents and letters. Apparently Major Fairbairn collected the boxes from the village store when he went for his provisions.'

Between the boxes were paths or passages to the table and the bookshelves. The window was shuttered and allowed little natural light to enter the room but beneath the window they could make out three trunks, their lids open. Between many of the books in the bookshelves were pieces of paper sticking out like flags; and here and there buff or fawn school exercise books. For several minutes both men stood contemplating the scene in silence.

'Nothing has been touched,' said Henry. 'That was quite specific in the will. Nothing must be touched before the heir comes.'

Mordecai remained silent. Then he shook his head almost in disbelief. 'I think we should have a drink,' he said.

In the kitchen Henry found two rough

tumblers while Mordecai, seated at the table, opened one of the bottles of champagne. He pointed to the hamper. 'Sandwich?' he said, pouring the wine. Henry pulled up a chair opposite him.

'Do you still want to stay the night here?' he asked.

'Yes, I want a good look at those papers.'

'You could spend the afternoon here and I'd collect you in the evening and take you to the hotel.'

'No,' Mordecai said violently. He thumped the table with the flat of his hand. 'I shall spend the night here, in my mother's home.'

Henry shrugged. 'Where on earth will you start?'

'Nearest to the chair – and the papers stuck between the books.'

'It'll take you an eternity.'

'I have until tomorrow morning,' Mordecai replied drily. 'I can make a start.'

They ate some of the sandwiches and drank some of the wine.

'I've recently had an odd report from the village,' Henry said.

'What was that?'

'One of my clerks, Jackson, was in the local pub. He overheard some talk about this house.'

'And?'

'Someone, Jackson gathered, had been inside the house on the night Roderick

93

Fairbairn died. That might have explained why the front door was ajar although the police thought it had been left open and Roderick Fairbairn fell when he was coming down to shut it. Then there was the broken window that I had boarded up. I thought it might have been like that for years. Because Roderick had died from natural causes, a massive heart attack before he had the fall which broke his neck, the police didn't investigate much. Nothing looked disturbed as far as I could tell from my earlier visit. But if the village gossip is right and someone had been in the house and Roderick had come across them, that might have started his heart attack. Could shock do that?'

'I suppose it might. Is there much crime locally?'

'Not a great deal. We get the usual youth trouble in the villages, and perhaps a villain or two from Bridport or Dorchester. I thought that the gossip in the pub might have been because some of the village kids had come and seen the corpse and run off before I got here. Apparently it was a game they played when Roderick was alive, creeping up here and spying on him. The hermit with long hair and a white beard. But when I found the body, there was no sign of any disturbance. No drawers or cupboards were open and the only odd thing was that the front door was ajar. If there had been someone else in the house, they could have left it open.' Henry paused and took a drink of champagne. 'I still think of the smile on his battered face when I found him. As though he was welcoming someone.'

'Perhaps he was.'

'Death, perhaps that's what he wanted. The wounds, the disfigurement, the death of his girl, he can't have been sorry for life to have ended. He was certainly very strange. When I came to make his will, he looked like an Old Testament prophet – or rather hermit, because he was as thin as a hairpin. I suppose he must have been suffering from heart trouble at the time when I was here.'

'Possibly, and he knew it and that was why he sent for you to make his will.'

'Are you still determined to spend the night in the house?'

'Of course. I'm not troubled by ghosts, if there are any, and I am very curious about the family papers. I hope to learn something from them, something about my side of the family, and judging by the sight of that library I shall have quite a search. So I'd best get started.'

'What will you do for supper?' Henry asked.

'Game pie, Fortnum and Mason's best – and some grapes. I'll manage.'

With the two unopened bottles of champagne to wash it down, Henry thought. He foraged in the dresser and put a couple of plates and a knife with a pearl handle and a spoon and a fork on the table. Mordecai picked up the silver and examined the mark and the crest. Grace's crest.

'Well, I must get home to the family,' Henry said. 'You're sure you'll be all right?'

'I'll manage.'

'The stove's made up. The hot water will last for tonight, although you may have to shave in cold water tomorrow.'

'I'll manage,' Mordecai repeated. He got to his feet and they returned to the hall.

'The drawing room is here.' Henry opened the door to the left of the hall and switched on the light. This room was brighter for there were two wide ground-floor sash windows, one boarded up. But the shutters seemed to fit more loosely than in the library and dining room. 'It's a fine room,' Henry went on. 'That's the window that I had boarded up.'

Mordecai stumped into the room. It was a square room, a cube with a fine cornice, a high ceiling and what was clearly an Adam fireplace, above which strips of wallpaper in the eighteenth-century Chinese style were falling in flaps. The furniture was covered in sheets on which the dust lay thick.

'The pictures are against the wall, also under sheets,' Henry continued. 'Family portraits.'

'I'd like to see them,' Mordecai said. Henry

bent and lifted the sheets and uncovered the pictures one by one. Three were of women, the most recent a portrait of a fine-boned woman in a high Edwardian dress, autocratic but handsome. Of the men, most were in uniform, starting with an early Fairbairn in a white wig and red coat. The most recent was a portrait of, Mordecai presumed, Grace's brother, for the sitter was in modern khaki with the red tabs and insignia of a full general, and rows of medals on the left breast. My uncle, Mordecai thought.

'Bring that into the hall,' he said. 'I'd like to take a closer look.'

He turned and left the room. Henry brought the picture and leaned it against the empty grate in the hall. 'I'll open the front door,' he said. 'That will give you some more light.' He opened the front door and once again the sunlight of the late summer afternoon flooded in. Mordecai examined the portrait.

'He's a fine-looking fellow,' said Henry. 'My uncle was very fond of him.' He watched Mordecai examining the portrait. 'Well, I must be off. By the way,' he added, 'I've left a torch on the hall table. I'm a bit uncertain about the electric light. The wiring's very old. Do you want me to show you the fuse box?'

Mordecai looked at him. 'My dear fellow,' he said, 'what would I want with the fuse box? I wouldn't have the slightest idea what to do with it. No, the torch is an excellent alternative.'

'Do you want to see me in the morning?'

'No. I've told Webster to be here at ten.'

'When you go, will you lock up and leave the key at the post office shop that we passed in the village? I'll collect it later. Then you'll have to tell me what you want done with the house.'

'I tell you that now. Sell it.'

'Easier said than done in its present state.' Henry walked to the front door. 'Shall I close it behind me?'

Mordecai nodded. 'The key's in the lock,' Henry said. And he was gone.

Mordecai waited until he heard the sound of the car driving away. Then he took the torch from where Henry had left it on the hall table and shone it on the portrait of the General. With the hall light he could see it well enough. He studied the self-confident, authoritative face. Why hadn't Grace turned to him when she was so unhappy?

He slipped the torch into his pocket and went into the library, making his way to the chair and the table by the empty fireplace. The passage between the cardboard boxes was narrow and with his two sticks he had difficulty negotiating his path. He reached the chair and sank into it, looking about him. The light from the single lamp cast shadows around the room. It was difficult to imagine that outside was the brightness of an August afternoon.

On the table to his right there was a pile of letters beneath a slim dark green leather volume with the title in gold leaf. He picked up the book and shook the dust from it. *The Fairbairns of Water Meadow House, Kingsford Langley,* by Maurice Fairbairn. A family history by the General? Mordecai began to read. And there they all were, his ancestors. So many soldiers, he thought as he turned the pages, fighting so many campaigns, killing so often and so many. But at least there was one lawyer, a judge in Madras in India in the nineteenth century. And there on the last page, just before the end of the family story, in the line beyond the General was Roderick with his date of birth. And also Grace. But there was no reference to her marriage – nor to her son.

He replaced the book on the table and picked up a handful of yellowing letters from the pile that the book had covered and began to read them. They were love letters, written between late 1940 and 1944, all in the same hand, all beginning 'My darling', all signed 'Anne'. He read more slowly than he had read the book partly because the letters were in manuscript and he had difficulty in deciphering some of the words; but mainly because the letters moved him deeply The passion expressed in them, the sincerity, the ache caused by separation, the longing for the end of war when the two lovers could be together again. He read them all, starting with those addressed to Middle East Forces when Roderick must have been fighting in the desert. Then, after an interval of months, the letters were addressed to prison hospitals in Germany, expressing relief that Roderick was alive, repeating her determination that they would get married as soon as the war was over and he was home. The final letters were written to the hospital in Liverpool when Roderick Fairbairn had been repatriated and Anne had seen him again. There had been no mention of his disfigurement in the earlier letters. Had he not told her when he had written from Germany? If he had not, her shock when she saw him must have been great. But nevertheless all the letters written after she saw him in Liverpool still spoke of her love, of her plans to marry. She urged him not to despair, telling him of the miracles they could now perform in rebuilding mutilated faces, giving him accounts of Archie McIndoe's work in the hospital at East Grinstead and begging him to go there for treatment.

When he had read the last, he lowered it to his lap and thought of the young man who had returned so disfigured and with one eye and one arm, so different from the young man who had gone to war. Mordecai thought of him sitting in the very chair in which he himself was presently sitting, reading and rereading the letters from the girl he had loved. They were very fine letters, he thought, especially those written after she had seen his terribly wounded face. Her words of encouragement, her message of hope, the promise renewed that they would marry despite his wounds because she loved him. She must have been a very special person, Mordecai thought. Then on the bottom of the last of her letters was a note in another hand. It said simply, 'Died on 18th June 1944, killed by a flying bomb in the Guards Chapel.'

He replaced the letters in their pile on the table and, leaning over the side of the chair to the box nearest him, he pulled out a clutch of papers. They were in a different hand from Anne's, Roderick's hand, more difficult to decipher, for they were written in almost a scribble, as if the author was in some desperate hurry. They were pages and pages of descriptions of battle and reflections on pain, a description of his wounds, and of his journey from Derna in North Africa to Athens in a hospital ship, then on the hospital train that took him, a wounded prisoner-of-war, into Germany. Mordecai spent a time reading these. They interested him but still they were not what he had come for so he replaced them in the box and, heaving himself to his feet, grabbed his two sticks and made for the bookshelves with the incongruous flags of paper and exercise books sticking out from between the volumes on the shelves. Leaning against the bookcase, his two sticks in one hand, he pulled out one of the buff exercise books and made his way back to the chair and opened it.

'I have the means to kill myself,' he read. 'That is both a comfort and a frustration. Since I came back here, I have always had the means to kill myself – from that very first day after I had left the hospital when I heard of Anne's death. For I have a gun, a nineteenth-century American .45 Colt army issue pistol which I bought from an old gunsmith in St James's Street in the summer of 1940 just before the blitz on London began.

'I had gone to the gunsmith to arm myself, for at that time equipment was so short after the losses at Dunkirk that the officers in the training battalion had no personal weapons and everyone expected the Germans were going to invade. We were being sent to the coast and I wanted to fight, as Winston Churchill had told us to fight, on the beaches. So I went to buy my own personal pistol. But that evening when I got back to the battalion, I found that that very afternoon we had all been issued with a modern 0.38 sidearm. So when I went to the Middle East, I left my American gun at home, hidden under some clothing in the room that was kept locked. It was still here when I got back. I took it out and loaded it, as at that time I intended to kill myself. I have kept it loaded, in the drawer in the table next to my bed. I take it out now and then and handle it. I keep it in working order so that at any time I can put it to my mouth and end this wretched existence. Only one thing stops me. It stopped me when I first came back here and it stops me still.

'If I thought that such a death would bring me to her, I'd do it immediately. When I first came home that is what I intended. Then there came to me a memory of what I had been taught as a child. That suicide, self-destruction was the ultimate sin, the gravest sin, the sin of Judas, and that the consequence of that sin was eternal damnation. Wasn't that the Christian orthodoxy? Anyway that is what I was taught. I don't know what I believe in now. A God that permitted the destruction of Anne must be a cruel God and I cursed him for years after she had died. And yet something of the old belief I learnt in childhood remained and held me back from killing myself. What I had been taught became very vivid to me. That if I killed myself then I might never join her. For if there is a God and if there is a Heaven, she's in Heaven. And were I to kill myself, I could never join her. I would be damned. So I have resisted the temptation and I have come to believe that if I lived out my Purgatory here on earth, I would get my reward – which would be to join her. But if I killed myself, I never would. So I have resigned myself to waiting until this wretched half-life comes naturally to its end. Please God, make that soon. What use am I to anyone here on earth, mutilated, disabled, still borne down by grief after so many weary years apart from her? And the possession of the gun comforts me, the knowledge that during all these years I have had the power to end my existence had I chosen to exercise it. Now I await my reward – that some day I will see her again.

'When I bought the gun, the old man said that years ago, in the last century, his father had bought it from an American who needed money to settle his hotel bill. The gun-smith said it might be ancient but that it was in perfect working order, which it was, and he threw in a box of ammunition as he wanted to be rid of me and shut the shop for like many then he was frightened. That night I spent with Anne in the flat in Kensington. This was a few weeks before the bombing of London began. A few weeks later when we lay together and I held her in my arms on my embarkation leave, the bombs were falling and London was burning. So the gun always reminds me of her and of that time of happiness despite the destruction and death that then surrounded us.

'My gun! My instrument that could at any time have ended my agony here on earth – but might, could, would, have taken me away from her for ever.'

The writing ended here. Overleaf were some poems about war and death, prayers, fantasy stories that seemed to have little point or purpose, almost, Mordecai thought, like the meandering and scribbling of an un-balanced mind.

He put down the exercise book on top of the family history on the table beside him. So Roderick had a gun? Was it still there in the bedside table in the bedroom, he wondered?

By now the evening had come. In what he now thought of as this rotting house peopled by unhappy spirits, he had read much about his unhappy cousin but nothing of what he had hoped to find. He took the torch from his pocket and played the beam on the boxes around the room. Where was he to turn now? The beam fell on one of the trunks beneath the window, a black cabin trunk, its lid, like the lids of the other two trunks, open. He read the inscription in white letters on its side: 'General Sir Maurice Fairbairn'. Grace's brother. That would be as likely a starting point in his search as any other. Perhaps there he might find some papers about the family.

He struggled to his feet and taking his two

sticks manoeuvred his way along the gap between the boxes until he came to the trunk. The light from the table lamp hardly reached this part of the room so, leaning on his sticks which he held in one hand, he took out his torch and shone it on the contents in the trunk. In it he could see bundles of documents tied together with tape, not the pink tape used for binding around his briefs, but faded white and green ribbon. He lowered himself carefully until he was sitting on one of the larger boxes. Then he bent forward and leaning over the trunk with his torch in one hand he began plucking at the bundles, rather, he thought, like a child bent over a bran tub searching for treasure.

Most, he soon saw, were bundles of ancient deeds or documents that Maurice Fairbairn had obviously used for his family history – lists of parish registers, burial certificates, marriage certificates, in some case King's Commissions and inscribed Mentions in Dispatches. Then near the bottom of the trunk, literally caked in dust, he found a bundle labelled 'Alice Fairbairn'.

Alice, he knew from the family history that he had earlier read, had been Grace's mother, his grandmother. The portrait in the dining room of the woman in the high Edwardian dress would have been her. He undid the tape around the bundle and started sifting through the documents. Some

106

were letters from her to her husband, another soldier, Colonel Herbert Fairbairn CB, Grace's father. Of these some were love letters; others notes, written when Alice and Herbert had been apart, relating to incidents of everyday life, all dated before 1904. The significance of that date he understood later. There were dance programmes with little pencils attached by a silver tassel; and theatre programmes of the 1880s. Then there was a birth certificate of her son Maurice, and many of Maurice's school reports; and Maurice's Commission, signed by the Queen Empress, Victoria. There were also several drafts of her will. But in all the documents in that bundle labelled 'Alice Fairbairn' there was no mention of a daughter. It was as if for Alice Fairbairn she had no daughter. That Grace did not exist.

Mystified, Mordecai put the bundle to one side and was about to turn his attention to the other two trunks when at the very bottom, in a corner, he found what he was looking for, what he had come to find.

At first he could not make out what was written on the grubby, dusty bundle, bound like the others in white, now grey, tape. He shone the torch on to it and peered closer. Then he made out what was written on the outside of the bundle. It was the single word, 'Grace'.

He resisted the temptation to slip off the tape as he had with the Alice Fairbairn bundle which he'd read perched awkwardly on one of the boxes. The thin Grace bundle was what he had come for and he would take it to where he could read it in greater comfort and at his leisure.

Moreover he had now spent the entire warm afternoon and early evening in the airless and musty library and he was thirsty. So slipping the bundle into the pocket of his jacket he made his way out of the library, switched off the library light and went slowly to the hall and through the dining room to the kitchen.

He turned on the light and dropped heavily on to one of the chairs by the table that bore the hamper – and the iced carrier that contained the remaining two bottles of champagne. He opened one, took a long draught, refilled the tumbler and, rejecting Fortnum and Mason's game pie, ate some biscuits. Then he took the bundle from his pocket. It was slight and very dirty and he tapped it hard against the end of the table to shake from it as much as possible of the dust and debris that it had gathered during the decades it had lain in the trunk. Once again he recharged his tumbler, then untied the tape and spread the documents on the table before him.

The first was a birth certificate; that of Grace Maria, born 28th December 1888, daughter of Colonel Herbert Fairbairn and The Lady Alice Fairbairn. Place of birth: Water Meadow House, Kingsford Langley, Dorset. Mordecai had never known the age of his mother or the date of her birthday. Aaron, usually so generous, never marked the day with a gift or celebration, either because he himself did not know it or more likely because Grace forbade him. Even Mordecai's birthdays had hardly been acknowledged by his mother. As a child he had never been given a party. Not that he'd minded for he had no real friends; there was no one he'd have welcomed. When he was older Aaron used to take him out for some treat, a visit to the zoo or Madame Tussaud's. But always it was just the two of them. Grace never came, nor when they returned did she ask where they had been.

Now, with the birth certificate before him, he knew her age. He began to think of her when they had lived in Tregunter Road. She would then have been only in her late twenties yet in his memory of her she had seemed much older; when they were in what she described as the 'hovel' in Lambeth and then when they moved to Cheyne Walk, she was still only in her thirties. Yet she had always seemed much older, older even than Aaron. Had she really looked so much older than she really was? Or was this only the memory of a child to whom all people seemed older than they really were as all places were larger? Then he thought of her pursed lips, her coldness, the few smiles, the absence of laughter. No wonder Aaron had turned elsewhere. Mordecai thought of the family that had come to Aaron's funeral. Where, he wondered, were those children now, his half brothers or sisters?

He put aside the birth certificate and took up the next document. It was a letter in clear, scholarly handwriting, written on heavy cream-coloured writing paper under the printed heading of The Headmistress, Mapperton School, Burford, Gloucestershire.

It began, 'Dear Lady Alice,' and was a lengthy letter, running to three full manuscript pages of closely written script. It was dated 17th December 1902 and was couched in deferential language, which however did not disguise the steely message that it conveyed. For the headmistress was making it very plain that the purpose of the letter was to give notice to Lady Alice that she required the immediate withdrawal of Grace from the school. Although the headmistress expressed regret, she wrote that she felt it would be in the best interests of the child as well as the school if Grace did not return in January

1903 for the start of the following term. Try as they had, the writer went on, the staff at Mapperton had failed, not so much to teach the child – that had been difficult enough – but to control her conduct. In her opinion, the headmistress informed Lady Alice, Grace would fare better in her home environment, being taught by visiting tutors under the vigilant eye and 'the closest and strictest supervision' (this was underlined) of her father and mother. What the headmistress could no longer tolerate was what she described as 'Grace's malign influence on other children in the school'. This, she went on, was the basic reason why she was taking so drastic a step, although she added there had also been incidents when Grace had been found in the possession of property of other pupils. She concluded by adding that she felt that this letter and message would not come as a surprise to Lady Alice, having regard to the discussions they had had over the past year concerning the character and conduct of Lady Alice's daughter. The only concession, as it were, that the headmistress made, in what was almost a postscript, the only good that she was able to report was Grace Fairbairn's talent for drawing and painting in watercolour.

Mordecai leaned back in his chair and drank some more of his wine while he read and reread the headmistress's letter. Then he placed it on top of the birth certificate. So Grace had, in effect, been expelled. Because of her 'malign influence'. That was a severe accusation to level at a child of fourteen. What exactly had the headmistress meant? It sounded as if it was more than just bad behaviour or ungovernable temper or the possession of 'other children's property', although, he noted, that had also been included in the headmistress's indictment. The adult Grace had certainly often displayed temper, as Mordecai himself had witnessed. But 'malign influence'?

His elation when he had found the bundle had now gone, as had his image of a young girl in a long, white Victorian dress running happily around the grounds of her parents' home. He turned to the next document.

This was a typewritten letter, from Coutts' Bank in the Strand, dated 7th December 1903, just a year after the letter from the school. It was addressed to Colonel Herbert Fairbairn and signed by a Mr Gerald Holmes, Manager.

'In accordance with your instructions, the sum of £300 in banknotes, together with a draft for another £300 dated 6th April 1904, were delivered to William Trench when he called here on 6th December inst. accompanied by Mr Henry Norman of Messrs Norman and Walters, solicitors of Lincoln's Inn Fields. The appropriate debits reflecting the above will be entered in the statement of your account that will be dispatched to you in the New Year.'

Beneath this laconic note was another, this time in manuscript, written from the offices of Messrs Norman and Walters, 6 Lincoln's Inn Fields, dated 7th December 1903. This too was addressed to Colonel Herbert Fairbairn and marked 'Confidential'.

'Yesterday, 6th December, I accompanied William Trench to Messrs Coutts' in the Strand, where he was handed £300 in notes and a draft for a similar sum post-dated four months later. On leaving the bank, my clerk, George Harding, as instructed, accompanied William Trench to Tilbury docks where Harding delivered to Trench the steamship ticket and witnessed Trench board the SS *Cumberland*, bound for Sydney, Australia. Harding waited at the dockside and saw the ship sail on the evening tide.

'I trust that this will prove a conclusion to this tragic business that has caused such pain to you and your family. I attach Trench's affirmation that doubtless you will want to keep with your papers.' It was signed Henry Norman.

Pinned to it was the following short document in typescript.

'In consideration for the sum of £300 and a draft for a like sum dated 6th April 1904 and the receipt of a steamship ticket to

Sydney, Australia, I hereby undertake to cease all communication, now or at any time in the future, with Grace Fairbairn.' It was signed, in an awkward, unscholarly hand, William Trench.

Once again Mordecai refilled his tumbler. There was little doubt what that letter and that note signified. An affair that the family had put an end to by having the young man shipped to the Colonies.

Grimly he turned to the penultimate document in the bundle. It was headed 'Memorandum by Maurice Fairbairn, Water Meadow House, July 1909'.

'I have been asked by my father to write this memorandum which he wishes to keep among his personal papers.

'In June 1903 I was with my regiment stationed at the Curragh in Ireland when I received a telegram from my father asking me to seek leave to come home on urgent family business.

'When I arrived at Water Meadow House on or about 30th June I found that my mother had taken to her bedroom and was under the care of the doctor. I was then told about the conduct of my sister, Grace.

'I knew that at the end of the previous year she had been withdrawn from her boarding school and that my parents, who were elderly, were gravely concerned about her behaviour and found her increasingly difficult to control. Apparently one afternoon about a week previously, my mother, who had been resting as she invariably did each afternoon, suddenly decided that she must go to the village to collect some item that she had forgotten during her trip in the morning. My father was out visiting a tenant in one of the estate cottages across the fields so my mother went to the stables to tell Trench, the groom, to prepare the dogcart to drive her to Kingsford Langley. In the stable yard there was no sign of the groom but she heard sounds coming from one of the boxes. She entered the stables and there on the straw in one of the boxes she saw Trench lying upon a half-naked Grace. My mother let out a cry and Trench turned his head. Both he and Grace stared up at her. Grace began to giggle. Whereupon my mother fled back to the house followed by the sounds of Grace's laughter.

'When later my father confronted her, Grace was quite brazen about her behaviour. She told him that she had lain often with Trench, that she enjoyed it and that she had done so on many times since the New Year when she had returned from school. She said, and said it defiantly, that she was carrying his child. It was then June.

'Subsequently my father paid for Trench to emigrate to Australia. For the last months of her pregnancy Grace was sent to a Mrs

Sumner to board in Devon where, in January 1904, she was delivered of a boy. None of the family was with her but a dispute arose because my parents were insisting that the child be put up for adoption and Grace was refusing. Eventually, after what my father called hysterical scenes between Grace and my parents, the child was taken from her. However before the child could be formally adopted, the baby sickened and died six weeks after his birth. At the time of the birth, my sister was hardly fifteen.

'My mother never fully recovered from the shock and for the last ten years of her life rarely left the house or indeed her room.

'When Grace returned from Devon, she remained as wilful and defiant as ever and my father said there were other incidents with young labourers on the estate but none with the consequences that had come from her relationship with Trench.

'As far as I could tell, on the few occasions when I was at home, she was mostly silent and sullen. When she was nineteen my father was glad to let her go to live with an elderly cousin, a widow, Mrs Winifred Houghton in Queen's Gate in London, and to study at the Royal Academy Schools. She never returned home. When she was twenty-one she came into some money left to her by our grandfather and she wrote, my father told me, telling him that she wanted no more financial help from him and that she intended to move into a flat on her own. She did not give her address, but soon after her twenty-first birthday she married Aaron Ledbury, a financier in the City and we never saw her again.

'I write this so that what occurred might be understood if it were ever questioned why Grace was not included in the wills of my father and mother. Signed, Maurice Fairbairn.'

To the last page of this document there was pinned the final item in the slender bundle marked 'Grace'.

It was a short letter, written from the Ritz Hotel, Rue de Vendôme, Paris. Mordecai recognized the handwriting. It was that of his mother, Grace. It was dated simply 1909 and read: 'This is to inform you that I am married to Aaron Ledbury. I do not wish ever to see any of you ever again.'

It was signed 'Grace'. But there was a footnote, a postscript.

'You murdered my beautiful, my darling little son.'

For a long time Mordecai sat, holding in his hand Maurice Fairbairn's memorandum with the note from Grace pinned to it. So he had not been Grace's only child. There had been another, a 'beautiful, darling' boy who had been taken from Grace and whom she accused her parents of having 'murdered'.

117

The existence of that child was the reason why Grace had rejected him, her second born, the cripple. During all his life she must have been comparing him with her 'beautiful, darling son'.

Then he remembered some words of Aaron when he was dying, words that at the time he had not understood. Something about Grace being 'experienced' when he had married her. Now he understood what these words meant.

On most evenings in Albany, Mordecai used to drink a whole or at any rate most of a bottle of champagne. On this evening in Water Meadow House, when he had completed the reading of the bundle marked 'Grace', he had finished a bottle. Earlier, in the afternoon, he and Stapleton had shared the first of the three he had brought from London. Now he took the third bottle from the case, opened it and filled the tumbler.

He picked up the documents again and reread them while he thought back on his early life, remembering year by year, step by step, all that he could about Aaron and Grace. The third bottle of wine was two thirds empty when at last he gathered up the documents, bundled them together, replaced the tape around them and tossed them into the hamper. As he did so, the kitchen light flickered and went out.

He switched on the torch, got to his feet and made his way into the hall. That light too had gone. Using the torch he slowly and with difficulty climbed the stairs. To his relief when he got to the bedroom and tried the switch, the bedside light came on, as did the light in the corridor. He went to the bathroom, washed his face and hands and cleaned his teeth. In the bedroom he pulled aside the curtain over the window, which was unshuttered and clear of creeper and open. It was a fine, moonlit night. Leaving the curtains drawn aside, he undressed and with difficulty clambered on to the high four-poster bed and lay thinking of Grace and of her childhood. Then he remembered what he had read in one of Roderick's scribblings so he pulled open the drawer of the bedside table. There, under a white handkerchief, he found the pistol.

He took from the drawer a large, long-barrelled Colt, the pistol that Roderick had bought from a gunsmith in 1940. Mordecai held it in his hand; and then he broke it and saw that it was loaded.

Suddenly the bedside lamp flickered and went out. Now all the lights in the house must have failed.

In the darkness he placed the gun on the bedside table beside the torch and lay back again, his mind full of his mother's child-hood, of her schooldays and young womanhood; and then of Roderick, her nephew. He wondered if Roderick had read his father's memorandum about Grace or had been told about her. Was that the reason why he had made Mordecai, Grace's son, his heir? Or was it merely because he, Mordecai, was the only member of the family still living?

Filled with these thoughts he lay on his bed in the darkness – except for the moonlight now and then streaming in from the open window. But he had his torch on the table beside him and soon he fell asleep.

Chapter Four

1

In the early morning a heavy mist hung over the water meadows and the river. Before long the sun burned it away, and it had turned into a fine August day when at exactly five minutes to ten the black limousine came slowly up the drive.

Webster had spent an agreeable evening in the bar of the Dog and Pheasant at Stoneleigh, chatting with the locals, talking especially to a garage mechanic from the village, and drinking perhaps a little too much beer. As a result when he rose in the morning he had a slight headache but like the mist it soon wore off and he was in his usual good spirits when he came up the drive through the dark tunnel formed by the overhanging rhododendrons, cursing once more at its awful state and fearing again for the suspension and axles of his precious car. He reflected how glad he was that he had passed the night in a friendly pub and not in this gloomy place. When the car emerged from the tunnel of rhododendron and came to the circle of gravel in front of the house, even the morning sunlight made the place look only a little more cheerful than it had the day before.

He pulled up directly outside the front door. It was open and when he entered he could see through the shadows of the hall the figure of Mordecai Ledbury seated in a chair by the table. He looked, Webster thought, like a hunched, saturnine Buddha – and the idea made Webster grin. He called out cheerily as he came into the hall.

'Morning, guv'nor. Bang on ten o'clock as instructed. I hope you had a good night?'

Mordecai did not reply but waved his hand peremptorily, signalling Webster to come closer. Webster saw to his surprise that he was unshaven, his face very pale and his clothes more than usually disordered. He's had a rough night, Webster thought. Serve him right for being so stubborn and staying here and not in the hotel.

'Take this,' Mordecai said abruptly, 'and drive as fast as you can to the village.' He handed Webster a slip of paper. 'At the village, telephone this number. You are to insist, I repeat insist, that Mr Stapleton come to me here immediately. Tell him that I need him and it is very urgent.'

'What's wrong, guv'nor?' Webster asked, startled by the urgency in Mordecai's voice.

'During the night there has been a shooting in the house—'

Webster interrupted. 'A shooting?'

'Yes. Upstairs, at the entrance to my bedroom there is the dead body of a man.'

'Good God, Mr Ledbury! What has happened?'

Mordecai did not answer. Instead he said, 'When you have spoken to Mr Stapleton and when you have made sure that he will leave immediately, you are to wait for fifteen minutes and then you are to telephone the local police. You are to tell them that when you came to Water Meadow House at ten o'clock this morning, Mr Mordecai Ledbury QC told you that there had been a shooting here last night and that there is the body of a man in the house. Tell them that I am here waiting for them. Do you understand?'

'Yes, but—'

'Remember to do exactly as I have said. Telephone Mr Stapleton first and then telephone the police. Do you understand?'

'Yes, sir, but what if I can't get Mr Stapleton?'

'Keep trying until you do. You must find him. If you really can't, leave a message that he is to come here directly. Then delay your message to the police by half an hour. I must have Mr Stapleton here before them. Now be off with you, and be back as soon as you can.'

'But you, sir? Are you all right? Shouldn't you come with me?'

'No, I shall remain here. You must make sure that Mr Stapleton is the first to arrive. I am relying on you. Now, do as I say. Go, and leave the front door open.'

Webster ran back to the car and ignoring now any consequences to his limousine drove fast over the potholes and away. Mordecai remained as he was, staring out across the hall on to the tangled rhododendron bushes. To his left, leaning against the empty grate, was the portrait of his uncle.

It was noon when Henry Stapleton's car drew up with a screech of brakes, the rear wheels flinging up the gravel as it came to a halt. He ran into the hall.

'I came as soon as I got the message. What has happened?' he cried.

'Last night or in the early hours of the morning a man forced his way into the house through, I believe, a window in the drawing room,' Mordecai replied, speaking very slowly. 'I was wakened when he came into the bedroom where I was sleeping. Some hours before, when I went to bed, I had found a pistol in the drawer of the bedside table belonging to Roderick Fairbairn. When the man came into the room, I thought he was about to attack me and I fired.'

As Mordecai was speaking, the limousine drew up behind Stapleton's car and Webster joined them. Mordecai went on in the same even tones. 'Go up to the bedroom and see for yourself. I need not tell you not to touch anything.'

Henry ran to the staircase and disappeared.

Mordecai turned to Webster. 'Did you get through to the police?'

'I did, sir. They didn't seem to believe me at first but I managed to convince them I was serious and they said they'd come immediately.'

Webster ran up the stairs and joined Henry who was bending over the body of a man lying face downward at the entrance to the bedroom. Henry straightened and Webster saw what was left of the man's head. He put his hand to his mouth.

'The back of the head,' Henry said almost to himself.

'Why do you say that?' asked Webster. 'Is that important?'

'It is,' said Henry quietly. 'It means that

the man must have been walking out of the bedroom when he was shot.'

He went to the stairs and stopped. 'Whatever happens, we must do all that we can to support him.'

'I should think so,' Webster replied almost indignantly.

As it happened, the Chief Superintendent, Thomas Blake, was at Stoneleigh police station on other business when Webster telephoned. He was standing by the desk in reception and the duty sergeant put his hand over the receiver and repeated to the Superintendent what Webster had told him.

'Ledbury?' said Blake, surprised. 'Did he say Ledbury?'

The duty sergeant repeated the question down the telephone. Then he said over his shoulder, 'Yes, sir, the informant says that he was sent by a Mr Mordecai Ledbury QC who is at the house. Mr Ledbury told him to report to the police.'

Ten minutes later the Superintendent and an officer in plain clothes, a Detective Sergeant Harold West, were being driven fast to Kingsford Langley.

'Mordecai Ledbury QC,' said West. 'Wasn't he the lad the Chief complained about at that conference a few weeks ago?'

'He was,' replied Blake grimly. 'Which is the reason why I am in the car with you. I

125

shall be interested to hear what Mr Ledbury has to tell us.'

Neither knew the way to Water Meadow House so they stopped at Kingsford Langley post office. It did duty also as a newsagent so it was open on Sunday mornings. It was from here that Webster had made his telephone calls earlier. West went into the shop to ask the way. When he returned he said, 'It's the house where Major Fairbairn was found dead a few weeks ago. The recluse, you remember?' He paused. 'The place is getting quite a reputation.'

'Like Mr Ledbury,' said Blake.

Twenty minutes later the police car drew up behind the limousine and Henry Stapleton's car.

'So we are not the first,' said Blake as they got out and went to the hall. 'I did not think we would be.'

Henry and Webster were standing on either side of the seated Mordecai.

'Police,' Blake said. Both policemen produced their warrant cards. Blake nodded curtly to Stapleton whom he knew.

Mordecai said, 'Webster, my driver.' He jerked his head to indicate Webster standing on his left. 'It was he who telephoned you from the village. There's no telephone in the house and no electric light. The fuses have blown. Upstairs in the entrance to the main bedroom is the dead body of a man. I shot

126

him with this.' He jerked his head and indicated the pistol that was lying on the hall table behind him.

'Take a look,' Blake said to West.

'I'll show you,' said Henry and he led West up the staircase.

'When did this happen?' Blake went on. He was standing in front of Mordecai looking down at him.

'In the early hours of the morning,' Mordecai replied. 'I don't know the time but not long before first light. As I said, there is no telephone. I cannot walk so I had to wait until ten o'clock when, as arranged, my driver came in his car to pick me up.'

'Do you live here?'

'No. I am visiting. The house belonged to the late Major Roderick Fairbairn. He was my cousin and he left the house to me in his will. The formalities of probate have not been completed. I came down from London by arrangement with Mr Stapleton, who is the executor, to look over the property. I also wanted to inspect the family papers. I spent the night here by myself.'

West and Henry returned to the hall. 'Shall I send for forensic?' West asked.

'I will,' said Blake. But at the police car, using the car's wireless telephone, he got through first to the Chief Constable. Only after he had spoken to the Chief did Blake telephone to order the forensic and incident

127

team. When he returned to the hall, he went to the table where Mordecai was sitting and peered down at the pistol but he did not touch it.

To West he said, 'Take a look around the rest of the house.' Then to Henry, 'Show me the body.'

They went together up the stairs. Mordecai called out to West, 'You may need this torch. Most of the place is shuttered.' He took the torch from his pocket and handed it to West. 'The man got in through a window in the drawing room,' he added.

West took the torch and went to the drawing room. Blake and Henry came down the stairs into the hall.

'You say you were in bed in that room?' Blake asked.

'I was. I woke when I saw the figure, the shape of a man and I thought he was going to attack me.'

'Why did you think that?'

'I thought he had something in his hand, a club or some weapon, so I stretched out my hand to the bedside table to pick up the torch and my hand fell upon the pistol.'

'What was the pistol doing there?'

'I had found it in the drawer as I was getting into bed. Earlier, when I was studying the papers that I had come to inspect, I had read in some of Roderick Fairbairn's writing in the library–' Mordecai pointed – 'that he owned a pistol that he'd got thirty years ago during the war.'

'Had you been looking for it?'

'I had read that Fairbairn kept it by the bed so I looked in the drawer.'

'Why?'

'As I said, earlier in the evening I had read what Roderick Fairbairn had written, that he kept the gun by his bed. He wrote that when he came back from the war he had been tempted to use it to kill himself, but he had decided not to for what might be described shortly as religious reasons. That interested me.'

There was a moment of silence before Blake went on, 'And you looked for the pistol and found it in the drawer?'

'Yes, I took it out of the drawer and handled it. Then I laid it on the bedside table.'

'Why didn't you put it back in the drawer?'

'Because just after I had taken it out of the drawer, the lights suddenly fused. In the darkness I laid the pistol on the top of the bedside table by the torch.'

West came back from the drawing room. 'The man got in through a window in there,' he said. 'I'll take a look at the other rooms.' He went to the library.

'Did you know that the pistol was loaded?' Blake continued.

'Yes. I had examined it when I found it.'

'In the dark?'

'No, that was before the lights fused. I could see the bullets in the chamber.'

'Had you ever used a pistol before?'

'Never.'

'Yet when you fired you hit the man?'

'Yes. I was woken by the door opening and stretched out my hand for the torch. I was half asleep. I thought that I was going to be attacked.'

'He has a poker in his hand,' said Henry.

'I saw that,' said Blake.

'I fired to frighten him off. There was only the moonlight.'

'You said you thought the figure was going to attack you?'

'I did.'

West reappeared. He had in his hands a champagne bottle wrapped in a dishcloth to avoid leaving his fingerprints. 'There are two more of these out there, all empty. Quite a party!' he said grinning.

'I drank some of it yesterday afternoon,' said Henry. 'Mr Ledbury and I shared a bottle with our sandwiches at lunchtime.'

'I drank most of the other two during the course of the day and the evening,' said Mordecai. 'What was left in the second bottle I drank this morning.' He paused. 'I drink a lot of champagne and I brought these bottles with me, as well as a hamper of food when I came here yesterday.'

'That's right,' said Webster, his first

intervention since the police had arrived. 'I took it into the kitchen, with the bottles in their carrier.'

'Three bottles?' asked Blake.

'Yes, there were three in the carrier,' said Webster.

'So you and Mr Stapleton,' Blake said to Mordecai, 'shared one bottle in the afternoon, and then during the course of the evening before you went up to bed you drank, by yourself, almost two bottles, two unopened, two fresh bottles?'

'I am accustomed to drinking champagne. I normally drink a bottle every evening–'

Blake interrupted. 'Two bottles,' he said, 'two full bottles, or almost two whole bottles of champagne were drunk entirely by you before you went up to bed?'

'Yes, I had discovered some papers about my family in the library when I was looking through some of the documents and I was distressed by what I had read. So I drank a little more than I usually do.'

'Was the effect of all that wine still with you when you saw the man in your bedroom?'

Mordecai stared at him. 'I told you,' he growled, 'that I am used to drinking champagne. I had slept for several hours before I was woken by the intruder who I believed was about to attack me. This was in the early hours of the morning. The wine did not affect me.'

'What did you eat last night when you were drinking two bottles of champagne?'

'Some biscuits from the hamper.'

'Nothing else?'

'Nothing.'

Outside a police car and a police van drew up, followed by an ambulance.

'Forensic,' said West.

Blake went out to the police cars. Again he got through to the Chief Constable. Then he returned to the hall and asked Mordecai if he had anything more to tell him.

'No,' said Mordecai. 'I have told you all there is to know. Now I should like a bath and a change of clothes, neither of which I can get here. I did not have much sleep last night and before I got to bed I spent a great many hours of a hot afternoon and evening in that musty library.' He paused. Blake said nothing. Mordecai went on, 'So I shall go home. Mr Stapleton will tell you where you can find me.' He turned to Webster. 'Webster, we must return to London. Fetch my case from the bedroom and the hamper from the kitchen.'

'No,' said Blake. 'You can go but everything in the house stays.'

Mordecai looked at him. 'Why?'

'Because I say so. Nothing is to leave until forensic and the photographers have finished.'

'Are you saying that I may not remove

132

even my razor?' he said.

'I expect you have another,' Blake replied, turning abruptly on his heel. A policeman wearing gloves removed the pistol, placed it in a cellophane bag and followed Blake.

Mordecai said to Henry, 'Will you stay while the police are here, collect my belongings and then later report to me?'

'Certainly,' Henry replied.

By now the house was filled with fingerprint officers and photographers. Upstairs the surgeon and his assistants were with the body, Blake and West with them. Mordecai beckoned to Henry and said quietly, 'Last night I put a slim bundle of documents, marked "Grace", in the hamper in the kitchen. The documents are very confidential, very personal. They concern my mother and they relate to events many years ago. I wish to take them with me and I don't want the police to see them. They have nothing to do with what happened here last night. Will you retrieve them for me?' He looked around him. 'I think they are all upstairs or in the drawing room.'

Webster followed Henry into the kitchen, keeping an eye out for the police. 'Is it serious?' he asked Henry quietly

Henry looked at him. 'It is,' he replied.

'But the man was a burglar!'

'I know. But he must have been shot when he was leaving the bedroom.'

133

'What of it?'

'He could not have been threatening Mr Ledbury when he was killed. He was leaving for he was shot in the back of the head.'

In the hall Henry handed the bundle to Mordecai who slipped it into the inside pocket of his jacket. He struggled to his feet.

'Give them my address in London. Doubtless they will have informed the press. They usually do, especially if someone notorious like me is involved. So it won't be long before the journalists are here. Come, Webster.'

He climbed slowly into the car and sank back into the rear seat. As the car turned in the drive and made for the road, Mordecai looked at the house over his shoulder. He said almost to himself, 'Unlike so many of my family who lived here, I'm not used to killing.'

'What was that, sir?' Webster asked.

'Never mind. And do not mind if I sleep during the journey home. I am very tired.'

Henry watched the limousine as it disappeared slowly down the drive. When it was out of sight, he went back into the house. Blake was standing by the hall table. 'The address?' he said, as abrupt as he had been earlier.

Henry scribbled on an envelope and handed it to Blake.

'Doubtless we shall be seeing him again,' Blake said, turning on his heel.

Doubtless you will, thought Henry.

2

Jack Edwards, a reporter on the *Dilminster Herald* whom the police usually contacted when they wished to leak a story, arrived at Water Meadow House just after the ambulance had removed the body of the dead man. Edwards was also a stringer for the *Daily Globe* in London so he rang their news editor to let him know that a man had been shot dead in the middle of the night at Water Meadow House in Dorset when the only other person in the house had been Mr Mordecai Ledbury QC. The news editor sent a reporter and a photographer to Ledbury's residence in Albany. The porters refused them admittance but agreed to take a message asking if Mr Ledbury would make a statement. No word came from Mordecai but one of the porters told the journalists that Mr Ledbury had left Albany on the Saturday morning and had returned on Sunday afternoon. He had been driven, as usual, in a hire car from South London Car Services. When Webster was confronted on his doorstep in Battersea, he told them that Mr Ledbury, who, as they ought to know, was a cripple, had been alone in the house and was asleep when he woke to find a masked

135

intruder in his bedroom. The man, who was armed, had threatened Mr Ledbury and Mr Ledbury had shot the man dead.

The story published by the newspapers on Monday morning was based mainly on the information obtained from Webster. It was a story of an elderly, crippled citizen defending himself from a murderous threat from a burglar.

The courts had risen for the summer recess and Mordecai did not leave Albany all Monday. In the morning he received a telephone call from Elizabeth Fanshawe.

'I've been reading the papers,' she said. 'What have you been up to?'

'Defending myself,' was the reply.

'Rather effectively, it seems. I'll come to London. Let's have luncheon together.'

'No, I'm not leaving here. The hacks would be after me.'

'Then I shall come to you.'

'No. Wait until it blows over. The rumpus won't last.'

'Did the police interview you?' Elizabeth went on.

'Of course. A superintendent. Not very friendly.'

There was a pause. She was thinking of the judge's dinner party. Then she said, 'You couldn't expect anything else, could you?'

'Why?'

'You know why. You weren't exactly polite

136

to the Chief Constable a few months ago. You made an enemy, remember?'

In Dilminster the slant of the press reports from London was noted by the Chief Constable with no great satisfaction. He gave strict instructions that the police enquiry should be particularly thorough.

The report of the Chief's confrontation at the judge's dinner party had percolated down to all ranks of his force. Many had themselves experienced pretty rough cross-examination by defending counsel, so the investigation into the death of a man at the hands of a leading QC was not unpleasing to them.

They soon established the identity of the dead man. He was Stevie Rouse, aged twenty-two, who had been brought up in Kingsford Langley but now lived in the south of the county near Bridport. As a youth he had got into trouble and had several convictions for minor offences, culminating in a sentence of detention to a juvenile institution for housebreaking when he had been just under eighteen. Both his father and his elder brother Jim had a police record. Over the past two years Stevie had been seen frequenting public houses patronized by serious local criminals and was known to go about with an older man, a Thomas Gooden who, like Jim, had several convictions for housebreaking and burglary and who lived on the same council estate as the Rouse family.

Stevie was reported to have known Water Meadow House when Roderick Fairbairn had been alive. The police also established that it was widely believed locally that the recluse Roderick Fairbairn had kept large sums of money in the house, which was full of silver and valuable paintings, and that since the death of Roderick Fairbairn it had stood empty. There was little doubt that Rouse had broken in through the unboarded ground-floor window in the drawing room.

Later on the Sunday morning of 26th August they found an elderly Ford Escort saloon parked in a lane on the borders of the grounds. The registered owner of the car was Thomas Gooden. When he was interviewed, he said that on the Saturday he and Jim Rouse had spent the afternoon at Warrenminster at a wedding party followed by a supper in the Bath Arms; that they'd got drunk and stayed the night in Warrenminster with his sister and brother-in-law. This the police confirmed. Stevie Rouse's family, especially Jim, appeared to be devastated by the death of young Stevie. Gooden told the police that on the Saturday Stevie had asked him for the loan of his car so that he could take a girlfriend to a nightclub in Yeovil. Fingerprints taken from Stevie checked with those in the Ford and showed that he had been using the car. The report of the post-mortem a few days later disclosed from the contents of the stomach that he had been drinking heavily.

The scene-of-crime team reported that two shots had been fired from the pistol, which was identified as an American Colt of .45 calibre, dating from some time in the late nineteenth century. The second bullet was extracted from the wood surround of the bedroom door.

The poker clenched in the dead man's right hand had apparently come from the library for it matched a set of fire irons in the library fireplace. The only fingerprints on the poker were those of Rouse.

A week after the shooting the police report was complete. Mordecai Ledbury was visited at Albany by Blake and West. He was asked if he had anything further to add to what he had said to Blake in the presence of Stapleton. 'Nothing,' Mordecai replied, and the police officers left.

The Chief Constable then sought and obtained an interview with the Director of Public Prosecutions, Walter Threadgold QC, in Buckingham Gate in London. He took with him Chief Superintendent Blake.

Walter Threadgold was coming to the end of his time in office. He had been appointed in 1952 so that he had now completed nearly twenty years in office. Prior to his appointment he had served as a lawyer in the Home Office. His had been a controversial appointment and it had grown more controversial, especially with many at the bar who privately accused him of selecting personal friends to conduct the most important – and thus most lucrative – prosecutions. By the 1970s as his retirement approached the bar was generally looking forward to seeing the back of him. But there was no denying Threadgold's sound knowledge of criminal law and his extensive experience.

It was not until the Wednesday week after the shooting that the DPP saw the Chief Constable and Blake. By then the story had gone from the front to the inside pages of the newspapers but it was still the 'silly season', when Parliament and the courts had risen, so it featured for some time after the first report. Background pieces told the story of the reclusive, mutilated war hero, who had died in the same house not long before Rouse's death; and the legal career of Mordecai Ledbury and his most famous cases were featured. In the press the pistol, incorrectly, was referred to as British Army issue, probably retained by Roderick Fairbairn from his service in the war.

With the two police officers seated in chairs opposite him and with the police report in front of him, Threadgold adjusted the old-fashioned pince-nez which he carried on a black ribbon around his neck and which, when in place, flattened the prominent hairs that sprouted on the brim of his prominent nose.

'Ledbury,' he began, 'Mordecai Ledbury. Well, well.'

Walter Threadgold, like many others, had once been at the sharp end of Mordecai Ledbury's tongue and he had never forgotten the incident or forgiven it. The occasion had been a Guest Night dinner in the Inner Temple in the late 1960s, which he and Mordecai had both been attending. Mordecai had heard from younger members of his chambers who practised in the criminal courts instances of the DPP's favouritism. At the dinner the two men happened to be seated opposite each other and, seizing the opportunity, Mordecai leaned across the table and said loudly, 'Is it true, Threadgold, that you distribute the briefs for all the major prosecutions to a small coterie of your pals?'

On one side of Threadgold had been the American Ambassador and on the other the Permanent Secretary at the Home Office. Both overheard Mordecai's question.

'What did you say?' Threadgold had replied, looking pointedly at the silver tankard Mordecai was holding. He had, of course, refused the chablis and the claret and the steward had copiously filled the tankard with champagne.

Mordecai repeated, 'It is said at the bar

141

that you give the best briefs to your personal friends.'

'I have no idea what you are talking about,' Threadgold replied.

'Don't you? I am talking about the habit that you have adopted ever since you have been DPP,' Mordecai went on equally loudly, 'of only using your particular friends as prosecutors in the big cases.'

Threadgold flushed. The Permanent Secretary looked grave; the Ambassador embarrassed. 'That is a most offensive suggestion. But if you knew more about the system of criminal prosecutions than you do, you'd know that only counsel on the Attorney General's list are selected for serious prosecutions.'

'And who gets them on to that list? You. Isn't that so?'

'The Attorney's list is a matter for him.'

'Well, I'm only reporting your reputation with the criminal bar. Blatant favouritism, they call it.'

'I have nothing more to say to you, Ledbury.' And Threadgold had turned away to talk to the Ambassador.

At that moment the Treasurer had banged on his gavel, the diners rose and the Treasurer intoned the grace: '*Benedicto benedicatur.*' Mordecai, unable to get so promptly to his feet as the others, was still seated as the diners filed off the bench table and into the interior rooms for port and dessert.

Threadgold was not a man to overlook so public a confrontation but Mordecai Ledbury rarely practised in the criminal courts so the two had little chance of encountering each other. But now Ledbury's name had emerged in a police report.

'Ledbury,' he said softly. 'Yes, I heard about the shooting in Dorset but I have not read the reports myself. I am not a regular reader of the popular press. Where did the weapon that was used in the shooting come from?'

'Apparently it was with the late Major Fairbairn's belongings.'

'Who was he, and did he have a licence to possess it?'

'No, sir. He did not. Major Fairbairn was a recluse and had been badly wounded and scarred in the war. He kept the pistol apparently in the drawer beside the bed which Mr Ledbury was occupying when he had gone to the house, he claimed, in order to examine certain family papers. For some reason Mr Ledbury found the gun when he settled himself for the night. He says that when he saw, or rather made out, the figure in the moonlight, he just picked up the pistol and fired.'

In the silence that followed, Threadgold continued to study the report. At last he removed his pince-nez, polished the lenses with a red bandanna handkerchief and said, 'An excellent report. Unless you have anything further to add, you must leave this grave matter with me. Let me know if any further information comes to light. Having regard to the identity of the person involved, it will be a matter on which I shall consult the Attorney General.'

The police officers rose to their feet. In the car on the return to the West Country, the Chief Constable said to Blake, 'I have the impression that was not an unsatisfactory interview.'

The administration that had come into office in the spring of that year had found difficulty in finding any properly qualified MPs to fill the offices of the two Law Officers of the Crown, namely, the Attorney General and Solicitor General. The Attorney was the senior, the Solicitor acting for him in his absence. They were the official legal advisers to the Cabinet and also to the House of Commons and at that time had to be drawn from lawyers then elected to the House of Commons and supporting the administration. The Law Officers also had other, non-political, responsibilities, representing the Crown before the courts, and the Attorney General was ultimately responsible to the House of Commons for the conduct of criminal prosecutions, answering in Parliament for the Director of Public Prosecutions – or DPP as he was generally known. In this part of his functions the Attorney General was wholly independent of the government of which he was a member. Ever since the fall of a government fifty years earlier brought about by allegations of political influence over a criminal prosecution, ministers and civil servants had been scrupulous in avoiding any perception of interference in the Attorney General's prosecuting responsibilities.

Naturally the vast bulk of criminal prosecutions was in the hands of the DPP, who was a permanent official. He answered to the Attorney General, who was consulted only when there was involved a substantial element of what was called 'public interest', although his consent was necessary to bring a prosecution under certain statutes, for instance the Official Secrets Act. But the recently elected government found that among the ranks of the MPs of the governing party there were no lawyers with distinction and experience in criminal law, in respect of which the Attorney General needed some experience if he were to feel easy in the conduct of the office. After much hesitation, Herbert Meadows, a Chancery lawyer, was appointed Attorney General and Philip Smythe, a Revenue expert, Solicitor General.

Sir Herbert Meadows was a mild, rather

diffident man of considerable intellect with a pleasant manner when speaking in the House, where he was popular with both sides even if he was not rated very high. But there was no doubt, as Walter Threadgold told his Deputy, that Meadows was, in both his private life and his practice at the bar, unworldly or 'not streetwise', as the DPP put it. However, as the DPP also observed, he did have sense enough to appreciate how inexperienced he was in criminal law so that whenever the DPP brought to his attention a question of whether or not to prosecute, he could expect that the Attorney would defer to him. Nevertheless in the few months since Herbert Meadows' appointment, the DPP had been punctilious in consulting him even when this was not necessary. He did this primarily to 'cover his own back', for it was obvious to the Attorney's staff, who were all lawyers, that in the consultations between the diffident Attorney General and the experienced DPP it was the latter who dominated and whose opinions were those that prevailed.

Accordingly an appointment was duly made for the DPP to come to the Attorney's room in the law courts at four thirty the following day. Sir Herbert waited for the meeting with the dread that he usually felt when the DPP sought an interview, knowing that it would be a matter about which he would have little to contribute. There would be no point in inviting the Solicitor General to be present since he would have even less and he was prohibited from consulting on such matters with any of his more worldly political colleagues.

The DPP was duly driven from Buckingham Gate to the courtyard beside the main entrance to the law courts in the Strand, was deposited at the side door and climbed the stairs to emerge into the long passage that led to the Attorney's large room.

'Come in, Director, come in and sit down,' began the Attorney affably, affecting a geniality he did not feel. 'What brings you here this afternoon?'

For answer, Threadgold drew up his chair to the desk behind which Henry Meadows was seated, and laid a file upon it. He then placed his pince-nez in position on the bridge of his nose and, clearing his throat, began.

'I have come, Attorney, about an important matter which concerns one of our own profession.'

'One of our profession?'

'Yes, a quite prominent barrister.'

'And who is that, pray?' asked the Attorney apprehensively.

'Mordecai Ledbury QC. Do you happen to know him, Attorney?'

'Ledbury? No, I have never come across him personally although, of course, I have heard about him. We are not members of the same Inn of Court and he practises in a branch of the law with which I have never been concerned, libel, I believe, and so on.'

'Have you come across him in private life?' The DPP removed his pince-nez and stared sternly at the Attorney. Meadows became even more apprehensive.

'No, I can't say that I have.'

'Good.' The DPP paused. Then leaning back in his chair he said, 'Then I must tell you that Ledbury is arrogant and often rude. But he has, as we both know, acquired at the bar a certain fame.'

Meadows was now struck by a thought. 'Ledbury? Haven't I read something about him recently in the *Telegraph* or *The Times?*'

'You have. There have been reports of a shooting incident in which he has been concerned. It occurred at a house in the West Country when Ledbury shot an intruder in the middle of the night.'

'Of course. Now I remember. An intruder who was shot when engaged in burglary and who had threatened Ledbury who–'

'Fired so accurately and so skilfully that, despite the limited light at the time, his shot penetrated the intruder's head killing him instantaneously But, and this is the significant point, Attorney, the shot that killed penetrated the back of the intruder's head.'

'The back of his head?'

'Yes, the back of his head. That means,' said Threadgold, tapping the police report with his pince-nez, 'Rouse, that is the dead man, must have turned and been going away from Ledbury when the pistol was fired.'

Threadgold leaned back in his chair. The Attorney understood that he was expected to comment. 'So the man who was killed had his back to Ledbury when Ledbury shot him?'

'Exactly, Attorney. You have the point perfectly.' The Attorney tried to stifle the expression of relief that had flitted over his face. Threadgold went on, 'And then there was the question of drink, which I think may be pertinent.'

'Drink?'

'Yes. The police recovered three empty bottles of champagne from the kitchen, two whole bottles of which Ledbury admitted he had himself drunk before going to bed.' Threadgold fiddled with his pince-nez at the end of the black ribbon. He knew that the Attorney was a teetotaller. 'We cannot say, of course, that Ledbury was affected by the wine, for it was drunk some hours before the intruder entered his room. However I consider this question about the consumption of alcohol important to the background of the case.' He paused. 'Ledbury says that when he fired the pistol, the man was armed with some object.'

'Armed?'

'Yes, with a bludgeon or some such weapon and when the dead man was found, he did have a poker clenched in his right hand. Then there were two shots. In other words two separate pressures of the finger on the trigger. One bullet struck the lintel of the door, one bullet hit and killed the intruder.' Threadgold paused. 'The bullet lodged in the doorway might, it seems, have been fired first, and it was the second shot caused by a second pressure on the trigger which struck the man.' He paused again. 'And that second shot must have been fired when the intruder had turned away and was leaving the room.'

'The gun, the pistol, Ledbury used. What was that doing in the house?'

'It was a handgun, an old nineteenth-century pistol that belonged to the previous owner of the house who had acquired it during the war. Ledbury claims that he found it in the bedroom. So we have an unlicensed, illegally possessed handgun and a victim who was shot by Ledbury, as he admits, firing with such accuracy that the man's head was almost blown off.'

'Shot in the back of the head?'

'Exactly. Shot when he must have turned from Ledbury and when he could not in any sense have been then threatening Ledbury who nevertheless fired two shots at him, one of which, presumably the second, killed him.'

'Oh dear, said Meadows.

'As I said,' the DPP went on, still staring severely at the Attorney, 'that night Ledbury had been drinking heavily.' He paused. 'Ledbury had apparently looked for and found the pistol, a relic as I said from the war which had been illegally in the possession of the previous owner of the house, now deceased. Having found it, and when aware of the presence of the intruder, Ledbury picked it up and fired at the man, obviously intending to kill or at least maim him.'

Threadgold paused and studied the Attorney, who was now looking even more troubled than when he had first welcomed the Director into his room.

'But the man, the intruder,' Meadows began hesitantly, 'he was a criminal, a burglar, and Ledbury was in bed at night. I always thought it was permissible to defend yourself and–'

'It is, Attorney, under the criminal law it certainly is permissible to defend oneself. Provided,' and here the DPP looked severely at the Attorney General, 'that the force used is proportionate to the threat presented. This certainly does not mean that it is permissible to shoot to kill when the intruder had turned away and was about to leave and when there could not have been any possible threat to life or limb.' The DPP

151

tapped the file on the desk in front of him. 'Consider this, Attorney, bearing in mind that the weapon was an illegal handgun. If the authorities do nothing in such a situation, what would the message be for a householder possessing, as many do, a licensed shotgun? Would not that message be that he is entitled to shoot to kill a person whom he has discovered breaking into his premises–' the DPP leaned forward again – 'and, moreover, that it is permissible to shoot to kill at a time when the burglar takes to his heels and is making his escape? No, Attorney, the law deals most strictly with those who take the law into their own hands, especially if a firearm is involved.'

He leaned back once more before continuing. 'In my opinion if the prosecuting authority does nothing over such a wanton use of a firearm, it would be giving the imprimatur, if I may use that word, to permit every farmer in the country to slaughter any petty thief found on his property. Agrarian crime, Attorney, is reaching serious proportions. If this incident goes unprosecuted, would it not be thought that we were giving citizens the right to take the law into their own hands and become almost licensed executioners? The countryside could be turned into a veritable killing ground.'

'So what are you suggesting?' the Attorney said weakly.

'That Mordecai Ledbury should be prosecuted.' The DPP paused, then added, 'For murder.'

'Murder!' the Attorney expostulated.

'Yes, murder. For deliberately shooting a man who at the time was not conceivably mounting any threat to him.'

'But, but Mordecai Ledbury, a QC, a–'

'I hope that a person's position would not protect him from the appropriate application of the law. The fact that Ledbury is a Queen's Counsel, a member of the same profession as you, Attorney, should not surely prevent him from suffering the same consequences as any more humble citizen. Consider the public reaction if you, or I for that matter, were seen to be failing to do our duty because the accused had acquired prominence in the walk of life that is shared by you and me.'

The Attorney shifted uncomfortably in his chair. Threadgold went on, 'That, I venture to suggest, might be easily seized upon by the media with disastrous consequences to your and my reputation as public servants.'

Threadgold stopped. He saw that he need say no more. At the mention of media criticism for failing to prosecute because of the status of the accused, a look of alarm had flitted across Meadows' face. After three months in office and after the critical comments that had been made on his appointment, he harboured a veritable terror of the press.

There was a long silence. 'Well, Director,' Meadows said at last. 'If you with all your experience consider that this is the correct course to follow, I will not disagree. But it does seem harsh that a person can be prosecuted when he was trying to defend himself.'

'The proper application of the criminal law, Attorney,' said Threadgold, picking up the file from the desk, 'may on occasion appear to be harsh. But a plea of self-defence can only obtain when the measure of force used to defend oneself is commensurate with the threat being used against oneself. Shooting a man in the back and blowing off his head is surely a wholly unreasonable application of any need to defend oneself. No, I am sure that a decision to prosecute in this case is correct. It will send a signal to every owner of a shotgun that he may not gratuitously slaughter any petty thief or criminal he finds on his premises. That I consider is the paramount public interest in this case.'

He rose to his feet. 'Technically a decision to prosecute does not formally require your consent, but as there seemed to be an important point of public interest here I thought it best to discuss the matter with you.'

And if for any reason anything went

wrong, although there was no reason why it should, he could always say that he had discussed the matter with the Attorney General who had approved his decision.

'Now I must not detain you further from the affairs of state with which I know you are so heavily burdened.'

And he was gone, loping along the passage, down the stairs and into his waiting car, leaving behind him a troubled, bewildered Law Officer who tried without much success to comfort himself with a reminder of the DPP's reputation and experience.

Back in his office the DPP authorized the prosecution to be commenced and telephoned the Dilminster police to make the arrest.

3

It was Blake and West who came to Albany to make the arrest. It was at eight o'clock on a September morning.

Mordecai had been given no warning. He opened the door dressed in his gold and red dressing gown with the embroidered dragon and specially made velvet slippers embossed with matching gold, the soles heavy and built up with rubber for his crippled feet. His sticks were crooked over his arm. Beneath the bottom of the dressing gown,

West saw the legs of black silk pyjamas.

'Mr Mordecai Ledbury,' Blake began. 'Detective Sergeant West and I–'

Mordecai interrupted. 'I know who you are and you know who I am. Don't stand there gabbling on the doorstep. Come inside.'

The policemen followed him into the apartment.

'Shut the door behind you.' In the sitting room Mordecai fell into a chair. 'Well, what is it?'

'I have a warrant for your arrest for the murder of Steven Rouse at the Water Meadow House on 25th August this year. I have to warn you that anything–'

'Stop.' Mordecai opened the drawer of the desk behind his chair and took out a tape recorder. He switched it on. 'Now go on.'

Blake looked at West. Then he went on, 'You have the right to remain silent but anything you say may be taken down in writing and may be used in evidence at your trial.' He stopped.

'You're a bunch of damn fools,' said Mordecai. 'This is a personal vendetta. Take that down. And write this.'

West produced a pad and pen. Mordecai waved him to a chair and began to dictate.

'As I explained to you when you came to the Water Meadow House on the morning of Sunday 26th August, I had spent the previous night alone in the house. I am a cripple and I can only move with difficulty. I was asleep in the bedroom when I was woken by someone entering the room. I could see by the moonlight shining through the open window that the figure was holding or brandishing something, some weapon in his hand, and he was advancing to where I lay. I was only half awake and I stretched out my hand for the torch on my bedside table. But instead of the torch my hand fell on the pistol that I had found in the drawer when I had gone to bed after I had read some of Roderick Fairbairn's writings. The electric lights had all failed at that moment and so instead of putting it back into the drawer in the dark, I had laid it on the table by my torch. When I made out the outline of the figure and still not fully awake, I grasped the pistol and had some idea of scaring away the intruder by firing it. I had no intention whatsoever of trying to maim or murder the man, although I feared that he was about to attack me.' Mordecai stopped. 'When you have finished I shall read it through and then sign it.' This he did.

Blake said, 'We are to take you to Dilminster police station where you will be formally charged. The car is in the forecourt.'

'Dressed as I am?'

'No, of course not. Please get dressed.'

'Not until I have telephoned.' Mordecai stretched to the telephone and dialled.

'Henry,' he said. 'Two policemen are here at this unearthly hour of the morning and they have a warrant for my arrest for the murder of a man called Rouse. I shall get dressed and then they will take me to Dilminster police station. Will you, please, meet me there later in the morning? Get the best man possible and alert the local judge that an application for bail will be made this afternoon.' He paused. 'I am playing a tape recorder and have recorded everything that has been said. I shall bring it with me. Remember that.'

He replaced the receiver, rose and, taking his two sticks and the recorder, went without another word to the bedroom.

'Leave the door open,' Blake called out.

'I shall do nothing of the kind,' and he slammed the door behind him.

The two policemen passed the time in silence, looking uncomfortably out of the window, walking round the room, examining the books and finally sitting.

It had sounded all right when the Chief had told them of the DPP's decision, thought West, but now it seemed rather different.

It was an hour before Mordecai appeared fully dressed, still carrying the recorder. 'Very well,' he said. 'Let us go to the car.'

As they passed the porters' lobby, he called out, 'Tell my cleaner when she comes to do the apartment that I have left on a journey to Dilminster.'

Watched by the curious porters, the trio went down the steps to the forecourt. Blake got into the car beside Mordecai; West by the driver. As the car drew out into Piccadilly, a photographer ran beside the police car which conveniently slowed allowing him to take a picture through the side window. The car then accelerated away, pulling into the morning traffic going towards Piccadilly Circus.

'Who, I wonder, was so thoughtful as to arrange that?' said Mordecai. 'Who, I wonder, knew that this morning an arrest was to be made?'

Blake remained silent. West shifted uncomfortably in his seat. The Chief, of course.

Mordecai closed his eyes. 'Since it is clear that someone is up to tricks, I propose to say nothing during this journey. I intend to sleep.'

Two and a half hours later when they reached Dilminster Henry was waiting for them. He had been busy. He stood beside Mordecai when Mordecai was formally charged. When asked if he had anything to say, Mordecai replied, 'I have given a statement that has been written down by Detective Sergeant West and signed by me. It has also been recorded on a tape machine that I now hand to Mr Stapleton. This whole process is totally misconceived.'

159

Henry took the recorder and said, 'I have ascertained that Mr Justice Wetherby who lives twenty miles from here at Stafford Tarrant is the stand-by duty judge. He is prepared to receive an application for bail at his home this afternoon.' He turned to Mordecai. 'If it is agreeable to you I have instructed Mr Terence Brady, the Leader of the Circuit, to make the application. He is on his way here now but he understands that you may not approve of him and–'

'He'll do very well. So long as he understands that at any trial I shall defend myself.'

All this was said in the charge room in the presence of the desk sergeant, Superintendent Blake and Detective Sergeant West.

'Is there a room where I can interview my client and await the arrival of Mr Brady?' Henry asked.

The desk sergeant looked at Blake. After a pause, Blake said, 'The interview room.'

When Henry and Mordecai were seated at the table in the interview room, the desk sergeant returned to the charge room. Blake had disappeared to telephone the Chief Constable.

'It's on the one o'clock news on the radio,' said the desk sergeant.

'They tipped them off, I suppose.'

West shook his head. 'I don't know, I really don't know. All I hope is that it won't turn into an almighty cock-up.'

160

In his room in the law courts the Attorney General was at his desk working at his papers. Philip Smythe, the Solicitor General, entered. 'I've been at the Inner Temple for lunch. Not many there as it's still vacation but they'd heard about the arrest of Ledbury.'

Meadows' heart missed a beat. 'Oh, yes.' He initialled a paper and placed it neatly on top of the pile in his out-tray. The DPP had warned the Legal Secretary at the Law Officers Department that the arrest would be today so Meadows already knew.

'Rather a critical reaction, Herbert. I thought I should report that to you.'

'Was it indeed?' Meadows picked up a paper from his in-tray. 'Well, the Director was in no doubt about the correctness of the decision. He considered that a prosecution was the right course in the public interest. And he, Philip, knows a great deal more criminal law than you and I, as I am sure you will agree.'

The newspapers next morning agreed with the doubters that Philip Smythe had encountered at lunch. Their general line, even in the tabloids, was one of surprise. Some even expressed outrage, and the reports went further than usual in commenting on imminent proceedings in court – perhaps because any proceedings for contempt of court by a newspaper could only be brought by the Attorney General and editors were confident that this was not what this Attorney would dare to do. The newspapers made much of the fact that Mordecai was elderly and a cripple who was in bed in an isolated house without a telephone and in which all the lights had fused when he was threatened by an armed burglar whose background of crime and association with serious criminals was also revealed. The view expressed was that for an elderly man in those circumstances to use the first means of defence that came to hand was surely understandable. To charge a threatened householder with murder because of his instinctive reaction was surprising to say the least. It was noted with approval that even though the crime alleged was murder Mr Justice Wetherby had in the early evening granted bail on the accused's own recognizances and that Mr Ledbury was now back at his home in London. The fact that the intruder had been shot in the back of his head was not mentioned.

The DPP, incensed at the reports in the press, telephoned the Attorney General.

'This must be stopped, Attorney. The newspapers are criticizing the prosecution and distorting the facts. They have gone too far with their comment and this is clearly contempt of court. You should institute proceedings immediately.'

'Thank you for your advice, Director. I shall certainly consider what you suggest.'

Meadows asked Philip Smythe and the Legal Secretary to his room. When the Attorney reported what the Director had said, Philip looked grave. At lunch again at the Inner Temple another Bencher, a retired judge of the Old Bailey, had approached him. 'I suppose there's more to the case against Ledbury than has appeared in the press because otherwise I'd have thought this prosecution a bit odd,' he'd said. 'Not that I like the fellow, but a cripple facing an armed burglar, what was he expected to do?'

Philip had also dined the previous evening with the Deputy Chief Whip and a few other colleagues when the Deputy had been wondering how long the honeymoon with the press that the newly elected government was enjoying could last. He hoped nothing would occur to change that.

Philip had wondered how friendly the media would remain if the Attorney launched contempt proceedings against them and tried to commit an editor to jail. The press would not distinguish between the Attorney acting in his quasi-judicial role and the government of which he was a member that had come into office with such a wafer-thin majority.

'It's a bit late to stop the press now,' said the Legal Secretary.

In the previous administration he had served the previous Attorney General, Sir George Hendricks, a bull of a man who had fought in Burma and always treated the Director, who had avoided war service, with considerable disdain.

'But,' the Legal Secretary went on, 'that would not prevent you from commencing proceedings against the newspapers if you thought it wise.'

'The Director seems to want it,' said the Attorney unhappily.

'It would mean a serious confrontation with the press,' said Philip. 'Perhaps you should...' he paused, '...take that into account.'

For a time no one spoke. Then the Legal Secretary said, 'Perhaps a letter, Attorney, from me warning the press to be more careful might be preferable. I could do that if you thought it appropriate.'

The Attorney brightened. 'Yes that would seem a most reasonable compromise. Yes, do that, please.'

The reaction of the editor of the *Daily News* to the Legal Secretary's letter was similar to that of other editors. He flung the letter aside with an expletive. 'To hell with them,' he said to the legal manager. 'It's a stupid prosecution and they know it. We'll keep on with the background stories and let them go for us if they dare.' He turned to the assistant editor. 'See that we keep a close eye on what goes on.' He knew that Ledbury had a retainer from the group for their libel work. 'Management,' he said, 'would not want old Mordecai in clink!'

Mordecai himself, after he had been charged, had spent the afternoon in the interview room at Dilminster police station. No one had dared to put him in a cell. Henry and Terence Brady had returned at 6 p.m., the application for bail successful. The formalities were completed. Mordecai thanked Brady. 'I shall defend myself, you know.'

'I know. I was glad to be of help. Good luck.'

Henry took Mordecai home and fed him champagne. When Henry left the room his four-year-old daughter in her white nightdress stood in the door watching Mordecai drinking his wine.

'You're very ugly,' she said at last.

'I know I am.'

'Does it make you sad?'

'Very sad.'

The child said nothing – and then ran to him. 'Would you like me to give you a kiss?'

'I would,' he said solemnly, 'very much.'

Three hours later Webster had arrived and they set off on the return journey to London, arriving back at Albany in the small hours.

'Thank you for what you said to the press

when they interviewed you,' Mordecai said as Webster helped him from the car and up the steps. 'It set the tone, which was helpful. An old cripple in fear of his life!'

'Glad to be of help, guv'nor,' Webster replied. If Mr Stapleton is right you'll need all the help you can get, he thought. Shot in the back of the head. That was the problem, Mr Stapleton had said.

4

In late September, two weeks after Mordecai's arrest on a charge of murder, servants in the Lord Chancellor's Department assembled in anxious conclave. The subject under discussion was Mordecai Ledbury, and his status as a guest at the reception known as the Lord Chancellor's Breakfast.

The start of the legal year on 1st October was marked annually by a service in Westminster Abbey attended by the legal hierarchy. At the end of the service, during which the Lord Chancellor read the lesson, he would lead the judges in their ceremonial scarlet and full-bottomed wigs, the barristers wigged and gowned, and the solicitors in their subfusc, across St Margaret's Street in procession from the Abbey to the House of Lords. There, in the Royal Gallery, was held a great reception – or, as it was called, the

Lord Chancellor's Breakfast. In pre-war days, champagne had been served; in years to come it would be wine. But at this time there was only beer or a rum-based hot toddy to accompany the sandwiches and sausage rolls.

Invitations were always dispatched early in the summer, and as every Queen's Counsel was always on the list of guests one had been received and accepted by Mordecai. Now the officials gathered to ponder whether an invitation could or should be withdrawn from a guest awaiting trial for murder. For Mordecai Ledbury would shortly be appearing before a judge and jury, and at the Lord Chancellor's Breakfast all the judges would be present, one of whom would have to preside at Mordecai Ledbury's trial.

'I assume,' said one official, 'that the fellow will have the delicacy and good manners not to attend.'

'He couldn't have the effrontery to show his face,' said another.

'But he might,' interjected the Deputy to the Clerk to the Crown, wagging his head. 'He might.'

Eventually they decided to bring the matter before their superior, Sir Gervase Mostyn, the Clerk to the Crown, the senior civil servant and the Head of the Lord Chancellor's Department.

Sir Gervase differed from most civil servants because he was the scion of a noble family; his elder brother, the Viscount, sat in the House of Lords. He was an exceedingly handsome man of immense height, with aquiline features and silver hair, with a presence that was guaranteed to overawe newly appointed Lord Chancellors as well as the other Permanent Secretaries who were the chiefs of the great departments of state, such as the Foreign Office or the Ministries of Defence or Social Security, all of which carried far heavier guns in the scale of Whitehall armament than those borne by the official head of the modest department of the Lord Chancellor. But as the Permanent Secretary to the Treasury and Head of the Civil Service used to say admiringly, 'Gervase punches above his weight.'

At the time when the deputation of his civil servants waited upon him to raise the perplexing question of Mordecai and the Breakfast, Sir Gervase had more aggravating problems on his mind. He was having 'new boy' trouble.

The new boy was the new Lord Chancellor appointed when the new government had come into office. He was an aggressive Welshman, chapel-going but certainly not teetotal, who tried to make up in loquacity what he lacked in inches. Once in office, he had taken to attending official dinners and dining too often and too well so that on these occasions he could not be dissuaded from launching into fiery speeches on subjects not remotely connected with his ministerial responsibilities. As a result Sir Gervase was receiving many complaints from the Private Offices of other ministers who objected to the Lord Chancellor's interference in matters wholly outside his own department. When the officials broached the subject of Mordecai Ledbury's attendance at the Breakfast, Sir Gervase was dismissive. He had more important matters on his mind.

'In English law,' he pronounced grandly, 'a man is presumed innocent until he is proved guilty. We have not yet altered our rules of jurisprudence in order to accommodate our European neighbours with whom our present masters appear to be flirting so daringly. If Mordecai Ledbury wishes to attend and poison himself by partaking of that unpleasant drink that the guests at the Breakfast are offered nowadays, that's his business.'

And he sent them away. But as they were filing out of his room he added, 'My guess is that he will. Just for the devil of it. But I don't see what you can do about it.'

And the Clerk to the Crown was right. Mordecai did turn up. He did not attend the service at the Abbey but was driven by Webster to the peers' entrance of the House of Lords, arriving just when the line of scarlet and ermine-clad judges were entering. He had the grace to wait until the High Court, the red judges and the County Court judges in blue had gone inside, but then he pushed his way to the head of the line of following QCs who had been marshalled in strict order of seniority, ignoring the protests of those senior to him who now found themselves behind him. His progress, moreover, was so slow that a wide gap opened in the procession between the tail of the judges and the start of the bar. When at last he came to where an impatient and testy Lord Chancellor was waiting, Mordecai ignored the proffered hand. 'Can't shake hands, Lord Chancellor,' he said. 'Not with two sticks or I'd fall down. You're looking tolerably fit. They don't appear to be working you too hard.' And he stumped on. The Lord Chancellor's face went a brighter shade of puce.

Once inside the Royal Gallery Mordecai shouldered his way through the mass of red-robed figures and other distinguished guests crowding around long tables piled with plates of food and glasses. A waiter from behind a table offered him a glass of toddy. He waved it away.

'Champagne,' he said. Told there was none, he said loudly, 'Stingy fellow this new man. Bring me a glass of water.'

A thin, elderly QC in his full-bottomed wig and black robes had followed Mordecai to the table. Mordecai now grabbed him by the arm causing him to splutter over his hot toddy. 'Is that Wentworth over there?' Mordecai said. 'What on earth is Wentworth doing dressed up as a High Court judge? You don't mean to tell me they've made him up! They've made Horace Wentworth a judge! They can't have!'

Wiping his scalded mouth with his handkerchief, the elderly silk, who had no idea who it was who had accosted him, replied nervously, 'I don't know him, I'm afraid. I practise at the Chancery Bar. He's certainly not one of the judges in our division. Of course, it may be that he–'

Mordecai was not listening. He had turned to others in the throng behind him who were trying to get at the food and drink. 'If any of you fellows see the Director of Public Prosecutions, let me know. The fool's trying to prosecute me so I'd better avoid him. Much as I'd like to thrash him with my stick.' Those around him, embarrassed, moved away.

As no one else addressed a word to him, he stood for a time silently surveying the crowd and sipping his glass of water. Then he banged down his glass, causing others to turn towards him. 'I'm off,' he announced. 'I need a proper drink and I shall get none here.'

He made his way slowly to the entrance, people standing aside for him. As he passed through the crowd Sir Gervase Mostyn, immaculate in black morning coat and black waistcoat edged with a white slip, was talking to Mr Justice Wetherby. From his immense height Sir Gervase could see over the heads of the crowd and noticed Mordecai's figure approaching the entrance.

'Ledbury!' he said. 'I thought he might turn up.' And he chuckled.

'I granted him bail,' said the judge. 'I hope I won't have to try him. He's an awkward fellow.'

'It's not a popular prosecution,' Sir Gervase said. 'But I gather that the burglar he killed had turned his back on him so he could hardly be said to have been threatening Ledbury when he was shot.'

By now the Lord Chancellor had completed his duty of receiving and was standing in the room talking to the Attorney General. 'There's Mordecai Ledbury,' he said, indicating with his head.

Meadows looked. 'Oh dear,' he said. 'Oh dear.'

'The press don't like this prosecution,' said the Lord Chancellor, 'they don't like it one bit. So you'd better be damn certain, Herbert, that you get your man. For heaven's sake don't have a balls-up. We're in enough trouble as it is.' And the Lord Chancellor turned away.

Webster was waiting for Mordecai by the police box at the peers' entrance. He helped him into the car. 'All right, guv'nor?' he said as they drove away.

'I put in an appearance,' Mordecai replied. 'Just to show them.'

He had, however, returned the briefs in the legal term that had just begun and from that time on he was scarcely seen outside his chambers in Albany.

Across St James's Park in Buckingham Gate, the Director of Public Prosecutions was studying the statements that the police had taken from the proposed witnesses in the case of the killing of Stevie Rouse by Mordecai Ledbury. He was engaged in delivering what he called his 'riding instructions' to one of his staff, Gwyn Vaughan, who would be representing the prosecution at the preliminary hearing before the local magistrates, the process known as committal for trial.

This was the procedure that had succeeded that of the Grand Jury. It was now a bench of magistrates who would consider the statements obtained by the prosecution and decide whether the prosecution evidence warranted sending an accused for trial. If they did, they would commit him to stand trial at the next assize. They could make their decision merely after reading the statements, unless the accused required that the witnesses should give their evidence before the magistrates in person and on oath. While these committal proceedings would be in open court, reporting of what was said in court was banned and all that could be published was whether or not the magistrates had made a decision to commit for trial – unless the accused waived the right to have the proceedings barred from publication. Vaughan was the DPP's representative in the West of England, a dark, grim-looking man who was known in the directorate as an almost slavish admirer of the Director and who had as a result enjoyed much promotion. It was he who would be in charge of the prosecution at the preliminary hearing before the magistrates. A leading QC would then conduct the actual prosecution at the trial.

The DPP handed the police file back to Vaughan. 'The statements from the witnesses seem very satisfactory,' he said. 'There is clearly abundant evidence to warrant sending Ledbury for trial. The committal proceedings will be a formality.' He polished his pince-nez vigorously and replaced it on the bridge of his nose. 'We'll have to await the trial for the facts to be made known to the public and the tiresome misconceptions created by the media to be disabused.'

He rose from his chair and began to prowl around the room, pausing now and then to look down at the traffic pouring along Buckingham Gate just beyond the corner from the wall surrounding the Palace. He stood for a time in contemplation. Over his shoulder he continued:

'What the media has failed to appreciate is that this accused, when at the time he was under no threat to his life, shot down another human being in cold blood – as deliberately as if he were slaughtering a dog.'

He turned and faced Vaughan who nodded gravely. Vaughan himself had never met Mordecai Ledbury but what he had heard of him, he did not like: his reputation of arrogant behaviour in court, of being rude to judges, of indifference to the Lord Chancellor and the Lord Chancellor's Department – and of only drinking vintage champagne.

'It is an important case, Vaughan,' the Director went on. 'It is a prosecution of principle and of significance for the maintenance of the rule of law. As I made clear to the Attorney, if we overlooked what Ledbury did, namely, shoot a man in the back of his head when that man had turned away and was offering no possible threat to him, and if we failed to prosecute, we could have every farmer or householder in the countryside believing that they were entitled to use their shotguns to blast every trespasser found on their premises. As you know, the public resents the recent abolition of the death penalty and if such shooting as happened here was to be condoned, the countryside could turn into a shooting gallery.'

Vaughan nodded and the Director noted

with approval the solemn look on his face.

'This was not self-defence,' he went on. 'It was the deliberate killing of one human being by another. It was murder.'

'You are so right, Director,' Vaughan murmured.

For a moment there was silence. Then the Director slightly hesitantly continued. 'Because I have always greatly valued your work in the department, Vaughan, I should like to say something to you personally. It is, of course, confidential, you understand?'

'Of course, Director.'

'This case is important to me personally. In a year I shall be coming to the end of my time as Director. I do not wish my long service to end with a failure.' And above all, he thought but did not say, a failure at the hands of Mordecai Ledbury of all people.

'I understand, Director. I do so agree with you that it is an important principle of the law that you are upholding.'

In Albany on the other side of St James's Park, Mordecai Ledbury was also receiving a visitor, Henry Stapleton, his solicitor.

Over the weeks Henry had grown fond of Mordecai and he could not conceal his anxiety over the seriousness of Mordecai's situation. He knew that the prosecution would stress the lack of necessity for use of the gun, and the position of the wound in the dead man's skull. He had made clear his concern and he watched as Mordecai read the statements. When he had finished reading, Mordecai pushed aside the bundle of statements and said, 'So that will be their case.' Henry nodded. There was silence for a time and then Mordecai continued, 'Well, I should tell you that I have decided that I want a full-scale committal, with the attendance of all the witnesses to give their evidence on oath.'

'You want to take a look at the witnesses?' Henry replied. 'But you know all of them, at least the important witnesses. They are the police, Blake and West, and you know what they are like. Apart from them there are just the technical experts, the doctor and so on.'

'I know, but I still want them all called to give evidence on oath before the magistrates.'

'But why?' said Henry.

'I have decided that I shall try and persuade the magistrates to throw out the charge.'

Henry looked at him, astonished. 'You want to try and persuade the magistrates to refuse to commit you for trial?'

'I do.'

Henry shook his head. 'But the statements are quite clear. If the witnesses give evidence, they're not going to resile from what they've said in their statements. On the face of these statements the magistrates are bound to send you for trial.'

'You're probably right. Nevertheless I mean to try. What are the magistrates like down there?'

'Country people, local businessmen, landowners, pretty orthodox. The chairman of the bench is Sir Leslie Harrison. He's very experienced and certainly not known for siding with an accused or for leniency in his sentences. He'd never go against the police and the prosecution and discharge a person accused of murder. And he has great influence over most of the other magistrates.'

'What about the clerk?'

'Francis Peyton. A good lawyer and well thought of.'

In the magistrates' court, the clerk was the only professional lawyer, for the magistrates themselves were all lay men and women. The clerk's duty was to guide the magistrates on the law – but the decisions were those of the bench alone.

Mordecai lay back in his chair. 'The magistrates have the power to dismiss the case.'

'Technically, of course they do,' Henry replied, almost angrily. 'But Sir Leslie and his bench are not famous for doing anything out of the ordinary. He would never dismiss a case of murder before it even comes to trial.'

'I've nothing to lose by trying.'

'It means that you'll disclose your defence to the prosecution.'

'They know what my defence is. It's in the statement I gave to them. And I shall waive my right to having the proceedings in private. I want a public hearing with the more publicity the better. I believe that the public, or a good part of it, is on my side, even if the law is not.'

'Then why not wait until you're before a jury?'

Mordecai looked at him. 'I've decided to take a chance. If we fail, as you quite understandably think we shall, we won't be any the worse off.'

Henry shook his head again but he realized that nothing he said would alter Mordecai's decision. Mordecai had made up his mind.

'So I want a full committal, Henry. Inform the prosecution.'

After more conversation and Mordecai had given certain other instructions, Henry left. On the drive home, he was even more despondent than when he had arrived at Albany.

Later, in the early evening, Elizabeth Fanshawe arrived. As Mordecai refused to leave his rooms, she had brought a picnic. 'How are you?' she asked as she laid out gulls' eggs and smoked salmon sandwiches.

'Well enough,' Mordecai replied.

'You don't look well,' she said.

'A charge of murder hanging over one's head doesn't make for many restful nights.'

'But surely they aren't going to go on with it?'

'Oh, yes, they are. The Director of Public Prosecutions is an enemy.'

'Someone you have quarrelled with in the past?'

'Yes.'

'Like the Dilminster police,' she said quietly.

'I know what you're going to say. That they are my enemies is my own fault. And you'd be quite right.' She made a grimace and he went on, 'The DPP believes he can satisfy a jury that the use of a firearm in the circumstances was not justified. He believes that he'll get a verdict of guilty of murder.'

'And if he does?'

'It's a mandatory sentence. Life imprisonment.' He paused and began to peel a gull's egg. 'Thank you for bringing these. I've come from a legal reception where the food was disgusting and the drink non-existent. I only went in order to make a show, to prove I'm not frightened by them.' He examined the gull's egg. 'I'd miss these in prison. And this,' he added as he poured the champagne.

'But I've read of people...' She hesitated. '...who've killed someone and not been sent to prison.'

'That's when the verdict has been manslaughter. There's little room here for a verdict of manslaughter. I can hardly plead diminished responsibility. I can't say I was abused as a child although my mother certainly disliked me. And I have no record of insanity, although perhaps you may think I have because of the way I behave from time to time. No, it's self-defence or it's nothing.'

'Well, I think it's disgraceful – and so do many others.'

'Unfortunately they don't include the DPP.'

They sat for a while in silence and it was dark when Elizabeth left him. There was a fire burning in the grate and he sat in his chair by the window overlooking the flowerbeds divided by the central path that ran under the glass roof the length of Albany. The lamps had come on.

That crumbling house, he reflected, Water Meadow House. It had laid a curse on his mother's childhood; now it had laid its hand on him. Was it wise, he thought, to defend himself? What was the axiom? He who is his own lawyer has a fool for a client! But he knew that if he did get someone to defend him, he would never be able to stop himself from interfering. He had needed Terence Brady to get him bail. He couldn't have made the bail application for himself. If he'd applied in person, that might have caused embarrassment for the judge and Wetherby

181

might have felt that he ought to refuse it. That it would have appeared too crony-like for him to have granted it. But Terence Brady was able to say things about Mordecai Ledbury that he could not say himself. Brady could and did speak of Mordecai's professional standing, of his reputation for integrity – and of his disability. That he couldn't run away even if he wanted to! None of this would have come well from his own lips. But it could and did from his counsel. So bail had been granted.

But when it came to court, matters would be different. Then he would have to speak for himself. He wouldn't be able to sit silent. He'd want to cross-examine; he'd want to make the speech. So at court he'd be his own lawyer, fool or not.

Henry of course was right, the magistrates would never refuse to commit him for trial. They wouldn't have the balls to throw it out. Certainly not someone like the chairman Harrison whom Henry had described. But all the same he was determined to make a show before the magistrates. In reality it was more for the publicity, the public sympathy that he wished to arouse than any real chance that the magistrates might be brave enough to refuse to commit. Then, when it came to the trial, he might – he might get a maverick jury who would have read about the committal proceedings and might agree with the media.

But he knew about jury trials. He knew never to count on the result. There were always the imponderables. The atmosphere in the court in a particular trial, the mood and behaviour of the judge, the skill or clumsiness of the advocates, above all the uncertain temper of the jury – any jury – who so often took quite irrational likes or dislikes to this or that witness. And in addition to all the imponderables common to any trial, he knew that he had no real friends among the judges, with most of whom he had too often quarrelled. And the police and the DPP were out to get him.

For all his bravado at appearing at the Breakfast and telling Henry he wanted to have a full committal and planned to invite the magistrates to discharge him, he was for the first time in his life frightened. The night spent in that ruined house, the scene of the shooting with the blood and the brains of the man spread on the floor, the hostility of the police, his arrest, all had taken their toll. And he recognized the strength of the powers aligned against him – and the weakness of his defence in law. He had, after all, shot that man – and shot him when there was no real necessity to shoot, shot him when the man had turned away.

He rose from his chair and went to the pantry to fetch another bottle of Dom Perignon. He took a glass from the cupboard but before he uncorked the bottle he went to the bathroom and opened the cabinet. At the back, hidden behind the harmless packets of aspirin and Panadol, was another small bottle. It had no label around it. He took it from its place and held it for some time. He'd take it with him when he went to Dilminster. Then he replaced it in its hiding place and returned to the dining room and opened the bottle of champagne.

If he was found guilty, he knew what he would do. He had the means. He would not, he could not, face prison.

5

On the afternoon of Sunday 21st October, the day before the committal proceedings were to begin at Dilminster, Mordecai was driven from London by Webster. He sat at the back of the car grim-faced, and Webster had the sense not to speak. So it was in silence that they headed for the West Country.

Henry Stapleton had invited Mordecai to stay with him during the court proceedings but Mordecai had declined.

'I'd rather be on my own. Find me a hotel some way from Dilminster where I can be quiet.'

So Henry had settled for the Royal Hunt

Hotel some twelve miles from the town. He had booked the only bedroom with sitting room attached, and also a single room and a place in the garage. The name he had given was Webster, who was to occupy the single room and drive Mordecai to the court in Dilminster on the following morning.

On the day before, the Saturday, Henry had run into Terence Brady QC at a neighbour's drinks party. Henry had told him that the committal proceedings in Mordecai's case were to start on Monday and he asked Terence where he could get hold of him next week.

'Why?' asked Terence as he scribbled down the telephone number where he could be reached. 'Why should you want me? He's defending himself, isn't he?'

'He is, but we may need you if we have to apply for bail,' Henry replied. He then told Terence that Mordecai had demanded what was called a full-scale committal with the presence of all the witnesses.

'He wants to take a look at them, does he? But they'll only be the police and the medical witnesses. They can't have any more than those. After all he's admitted the shooting and there are no other witnesses to that.'

Henry told him what Mordecai had in mind. Terence gave a low whistle. 'But the police have surely enough to get a committal.'

'He plans to invite the magistrates to discharge him.'

Terence looked at Henry, astounded. 'Not a hope in hell. They'll never do that, certainly not any bench with Leslie Harrison presiding. Harrison would never throw out a prosecution application for a committal for trial for murder. It would be lunacy to try. He should wait until he has a jury.'

'I know,' Henry replied morosely, 'but it's what Mordecai has demanded. I am scared that Harrison might become so irritated that when the time comes for the continuance for bail, he would get awkward. And then I'll have to call on you to apply to the judge.'

It was growing dark when Webster, following the instructions Henry had given him, swung the car into the drive and pulled up opposite the entrance to the Royal Hunt Hotel. Henry met them in the hall.

'Any sign of any hacks?' Mordecai asked.

'Not so far, but it probably won't be long before they turn up. There's a message from John Plater of the *Daily News*. He said he'd be here at six thirty.'

'Alone?'

'I hope so.'

They went up to the sitting room, Webster bringing Mordecai's bag and the carrier which held his supply of champagne. When Webster had left them, Mordecai opened a

186

bottle and offered a glass to Henry who shook his head.

'Ring down for what you want,' Mordecai said.

'No, thank you.'

'All the more then for John Plater and me. Do you remember what Max Beaverbrook said about Arnold Bennett?' Henry shook his head. 'He said, "Oh, how I love my Arnold and how Arnold loves my champagne." Mordecai drank from his glass. 'Plater's a good man and there's not much that goes on in Fleet Street that escapes him. I have a retainer for the *News* and do all their libel work so I have worked with him before.'

'And the *News* has been pretty sympathetic so far. Why do you want to talk to him now?'

'To make sure he'll keep up the good work. Even if we get lucky, we'll need their support to stop Threadgold seeking a bill of indictment which he could if the magistrates throw it out.' He looked at Henry. 'I know,' he went on, 'I know, it's a long shot but it's worth a try and in any event I want to get as much publicity as possible. I want public opinion on my side even if the law is not.'

'You can be sure that Harrison will keep a very tight control. He won't let you get away with anything, especially nothing against the police.'

'I've had a great deal of experience in

handling hostile judges,' Mordecai replied.

Perhaps you have when you were counsel, Henry thought, but not when you have been the accused. With Harrison as the chairman of the bench there was no chance the magistrates would dismiss the charge.

Mordecai asked him, 'Have you got the statement I asked you to get?'

'I have, and he's signed it. His name is Taylor.'

'Have the police interviewed him?'

'They have, some time ago.'

'How many shots does he speak about?'

'His statement only refers to one, although you say that you fired twice in rapid succession.'

Henry handed Mordecai the statement. Mordecai read it. When he had finished, he said, 'Was it signed in your presence?'

'It was.'

'And you'll make sure that he is there?'

Henry nodded. Mordecai put the document away in his briefcase. The telephone rang. Henry answered it, replaced the receiver and said, 'I'll go and fetch him.'

Shortly afterwards Henry showed into the room John Plater, a short dark man with what is known as an expensive face and a genial manner, and the three of them settled down to talk.

Chapter Five

1

It was the old courthouse that was used, an ancient and historic building that had witnessed countless trials since the seventeenth century. It had a timbered roof and whitewashed walls and the bench for the judge was raised so high that it dominated the court. In its centre was the judge's chair, placed beneath the faded colours of a Royal Coat of Arms painted on the wall. To the right of the bench and below it was the witness box, reached by several steps well worn over the centuries by scores of feet. Facing it across the well of the court, in which stood the broad oak table where the advocates sat, was the dock with short iron spikes protruding from the tops of three of its wooden sides. Only the side that backed on to the rear of the court was free of these.

On the walls were tablets on which were inscribed the names of famous judges who had presided in this court. Among them was Sir George Jeffreys who from that bench had sentenced to death or to transportation to the Colonies the former soldiers of the ragged army gathered in 1685 by the Duke of Monmouth in his ill-starred rebellion against his uncle, King James II. For Dilminster had been one of the courts visited by Chief Justice Jeffreys in the course of what came to be known as 'the Bloody Assizes'. The courtroom was also famous for a trial seventy years earlier at the very end of the nineteenth century that was still talked about by some who had been children at the time – the trial of a woman whom the townsfolk believed was a witch. She had been very old and so small that when she stood nothing could be seen of her above the wooden walls of the dock except her wizened face and long white locks. The summer heat on the day of her trial was oppressive. Rumbles of thunder began and soon became louder. As the clerk rose to ask her, 'How do you plead, guilty or not guilty?' there was a blinding flash of lightning and a crash of thunder – and the accused in the dock disappeared. The judge rose from his seat; cries rang out from the spectators; the clerk and the usher shouted for order; the court was lit by more flashes of lightning. Eventually the bent head and shoulders of the accused slowly rose above the sides of the dock.

The trapdoor in the dock that led to the steps up which prisoners were brought from the cells had not been properly secured and she had been catapulted down to the steps below. The old woman was accused of stealing herbs from a neighbour's garden and despite the efforts of the judge who at the end of the evidence practically directed then to acquit, the West Country jury brought in a verdict of guilty without even leaving the jury box. To their horror, the judge then sentenced her to one day's imprisonment and she was immediately released. She stumbled out of the courthouse between ranks of silent, hostile onlookers. Outside she was greeted with hisses from a small crowd as she tottered slowly down the cobbled street to her cottage.

This, then, was the court, redolent with atmosphere and history but much larger than the room usually used by the magistrates, that the Clerk to the Justices, anticipating the extent of public and press interest, had secured for the committal proceedings in the case of R. v. Ledbury.

'Most appropriate,' Mordecai had declared when he heard where the proceedings were to be held. 'We shall need all the witchcraft we can summon.' But he asked Henry Stapleton to see that he was not placed in the dock. 'I don't trust that trapdoor,' he said.

So Henry had arranged with the magistrates' clerk, Francis Peyton, that the accused, because of his disability and because these were only committal proceedings, should be permitted to sit with his solicitor at the table used for the advocates below the bench.

On the morning of Monday 22nd October the court was packed to overflowing with every seat taken. On the bench instead of one chair for the judge there were three for the magistrates. Henry Stapleton seated himself at the advocates' table in the well of the court; beside him stood Mordecai, bent forward, leaning on his sticks. Gwyn Vaughan, dressed in a black suit and a black tie, pushed through the spectators as he came from the advocates' robing room.

On the night before, mindful of his instructions from the Director and the Director's wishes, he had written out, word for word, what he would say in his opening address to the magistrates. He approached the advocates' table. Mordecai, standing by the table, barred his way to his seat.

'If you please, if you please,' Vaughan said tartly.

Mordecai glared at him. 'Who are you?'

'Vaughan, representing the Crown.'

'You're late.'

'I certainly am not,' Vaughan replied indignantly. He began to squeeze between Mordecai and the table.

'Don't barge,' cried Mordecai, 'or you'll have me over.'

'Then make room.'

Vaughan squeezed past Mordecai, then Henry, and took his seat. As he opened his file he heard Mordecai mutter, 'Clumsy oaf!' Vaughan looked up angrily but said nothing.

The curtains across the door at the back of the bench were drawn aside. All rose and through the very door that Judge Jeffreys had come to try Monmouth's rebels three hundred years before, the magistrates entered. The first to appear was a square, ruddy-faced, elderly man in a dark suit and regimental tie and high starched collar; next came a middle-aged woman dressed in purple. She was plump and matronly with a fine head of silver hair and steel-framed spectacles. The last of the three was a younger man, tall and thin, perhaps in his thirties, wearing a grey, Prince of Wales check suit and a loud jazzy tie. Behind them came Francis Peyton, the clerk. Henry excitedly grabbed Mordecai's sleeve. 'It's not Harrison,' he whispered. 'We're in luck.'

All took their seats. The magistrate in the centre looked round the court, nodding as if to friends. Then he said jovially, 'Good morning, everybody.'

Mordecai turned and bent towards Henry and whispered, 'If it's not Harrison, the man you warned me about, who is it?'

'Colonel Musgrove – rather unconventional, never quite know what he'll say or do. Quite a maverick.'

'And the others?' Mordecai asked.

'I don't know the woman; the younger man is called Southern. At least we've not got Harrison.'

We've a chance now without Harrison, Henry thought. Not much, but still a chance. Anyone was better than Harrison.

'Who's responsible for selecting the bench?'

'The clerk, Francis Peyton.'

Francis Peyton, who had now taken his place in a seat immediately below the magistrates' bench, was a solicitor with a voluminous knowledge of Petty Sessional law. Indeed he had acquired the reputation in the county of knowing almost by heart Stone's Justices Manual, the thick, blue-bound textbook that was the bible of Petty Sessional jurisdiction. He was a grey-haired, rather reserved man who in 1944 had been wounded in the leg in Normandy so that ever after he walked with a pronounced limp. In 1963 he had moved to Dilminster from London to live with his older sister in a small house in a village near Stoneleigh, leaving his wife in a home in Ealing where she was regularly visited by her husband. It was understood that she suffered from some mental problem, believed to be premature senility, or what later came to be known as Alzheimer's.

On arrival in Dilminster Francis had joined a local law practice and acquired a reputation for his expertise in the jurisdiction exercised by the magistrates. It was, therefore, to universal satisfaction that when the post of Clerk to the Justices became vacant in 1969 he was appointed. He was soon much relied upon by the Dilminster magistrates.

In September he had read in the newspapers about the arrest of Mordecai Ledbury on a charge of murder following the shooting of an intruder and he realized that in the near future Dilminster justices would be called on to effect committal for trial. Later the DPP's representative in the West Country, Gwyn Vaughan, had served on him the statements of the witnesses that the prosecution intended to call. He understood, Vaughan told Francis, that Mordecai Ledbury would be defending himself but that he had Henry Stapleton to help him. In Vaughan's opinion the committal proceedings would be a mere formality.

A little later Henry Stapleton visited him. 'My client,' Henry began, 'wishes to have a full committal with all the witnesses called before the magistrates.'

'I understood from Vaughan that committal would be a mere formality,' Francis replied, surprised.

'So did we all, but Mordecai wants the witnesses to be present to give their evidence on oath.'

'To take a look at them?' Francis asked.

Henry shrugged but said nothing. Francis walked to his desk. 'Isn't committal for trial a bit premature for a battle?' he said.

Henry merely repeated that Mordecai wanted a full committal with all the witnesses giving their evidence in person.

Francis then telephoned Vaughan, who in turn spoke to the DPP.

'Just like Ledbury!' Threadgold said. 'A full hearing at committal is a waste of time and money. But at least, Vaughan, it will give you the opportunity of clearing the minds of the magistrates from the misconceptions that some of the press have been putting about.'

Francis's next task had been to arrange for a bench of three Dilminster magistrates and set a date for the hearing. But before he did and mindful of what Henry Stapleton had told him, he read with great care the statements of the witnesses that the prosecution intended to call, including the statement Mordecai had given to the police giving his version of what had happened. That an advocate with the experience of Mordecai Ledbury wished to have the attendance of the witnesses must mean that the committal was not going to be a mere formality. So he thought long and hard over which of the Justices to select.

Then he arranged to see the chairman of

the Dilminster bench, Sir Leslie Harrison. Harrison, a local landowner, had been chairman of the bench for ten years. He valued his position and, some thought, overvalued his importance. As Henry had warned Mordecai, Harrison had the reputation of being a magistrate not likely often to favour the cause of any defendant and as a result he was liked and admired by local prosecutors and the police. After Francis had said on the telephone that he would like to talk about the Ledbury case, Sir Leslie received him with pleasure. He was looking forward to the prominence that must come his way as the chairman of the magistrates deputed to consider committing the case for trial. The Ledbury case would attract national publicity and even if the proceedings before his bench would be little more than a formality, some of the public interest and public notice would necessarily fall on him and the Dilminster bench. He was not aware that the defence required a full-scale hearing with the attendance of all the witnesses. If he had been, he would have been even more dismayed when he heard what the Clerk to the Justices had come to tell him.

For when Francis was shown into Sir Leslie's library, he began, 'Chairman, the committal in the Ledbury case will inevitably be a high profile occasion. It is bound to receive much attention in the press and I am concerned about your personal position.'

'My personal position?' Sir Leslie was surprised. 'What do you mean?'

'I understood that you and General Maurice Fairbairn had a family connection?'

'Yes, a very distant one. Many years ago a cousin of his married a cousin of mine. But what has that to do with it? Maurice Fairbairn died thirty years ago, in 1940.'

'I appreciate that but the house, Water Meadow House, where the shooting, the alleged murder, took place was where Maurice's son Roderick died and–'

'The fellow who came back from the war and became a recluse? No one ever saw him. I certainly did not.'

'I am sure you didn't, but the so-called murder weapon was a pistol owned by Roderick Fairbairn who kept it in the house which on his death he bequeathed to his first cousin, the accused Mordecai Ledbury.'

'Whom also I have never met.'

'No, but the fact remains that Ledbury must be a connection of yours, perhaps distant but nevertheless a connection. It is this that disturbs me.' Francis paused, looking grave. 'I would not want you to be in any way embarrassed or tainted by the family connection, however distant. In a case as notorious as this, the press is bound to dig into everyone's background. They would soon discover the family connection and I wouldn't want your position as chairman of the bench which you have served for so many years with such distinction to be in any way compromised.'

For a time Sir Leslie said nothing. He certainly did take seriously his service on the Dilminster bench and he particularly enjoyed his position as chairman. The last thing he wanted was for that to be compromised. 'Do you really think it might?' he asked.

'You know what the press are like, especially the tabloids. Some at present are very hostile to this prosecution and they would be bound to discover that there is a link between the Fairbairn family and you. After all, the accused, Ledbury, must be half a Fairbairn.'

Sir Leslie got up from his chair and walked around the room. 'Are you suggesting seriously that I ought not to sit? The committal will surely be a mere formality.'

Francis did not reply to this directly but said, 'Having regard to the sensational nature of the case, even the slightest connection could be distorted. The press is certainly capable of suggesting that your connection might in one or the other way lead to some improper influence, while others might consider that not to disqualify yourself in these circumstances showed a lack of judgement. So I am sure, Chairman, that it would be in your best interests to allow one of your deputies to preside. It would be most unfortunate if after all your years of service to the bench you became the subject of criticism.'

When Francis Peyton drove away in his small car he left behind him a much-disappointed chairman.

Francis's next call was upon one of the deputy chairmen, a senior magistrate, Colonel Harold Musgrove. He was a widower who had written several books about the Middle East where he had served for many years, and he was considered something of an orientalist. His hobby was bird watching. But he was not popular with his neighbours, some of whom considered his views eccentric, for Henry Musgrove had publicly supported the abolition of the death penalty, chaired meetings in favour of the Common Market and an ever closer association with Europe, and most eccentric of all, he would not allow the local Hunt to cross his land. On the bench, as in everything, he was no respecter of persons, informal in manner with a bluff, no-nonsense approach. He did what he thought was sensible and didn't care a damn for any appellate court or for the Lord Chancellor.

When Francis informed him of the chairman's decision to disqualify himself in the Ledbury case and invited him to preside, the clerk's approach was somewhat different to that which he had adopted with Sir Leslie. There was no mention that the committal proceedings could be a mere formality. Rather Francis told Harold Musgrove that the task he and his fellow magistrates would have to undertake would be an important exercise of judgement, requiring the careful examination of the evidence of the witnesses. He would need, Francis said, to have the best assistance that the Dilminster bench could provide.

'Someone a little more conventional, is that what you mean?' Musgrove smiled.

'No, of course not, but you ought to have a woman on the bench with you and I recommend Mrs Joan Whitfield,' Francis went on. 'She's the widow of a former General Secretary of the Trades Union Congress. She's a newcomer to the area, which would be an advantage, and she's only recently moved from London where she served for many years on the Ealing bench.'

'I'd heard she'd moved down here. But she's new in the neighbourhood and if as you say there'll be a lot of press interest, might it not be a mistake to have someone unknown on the bench?' asked Musgrove.

'She's a very experienced magistrate. She's been a Justice of the Peace for many years but has not yet sat at Dilminster for I have only recently arranged for her magistracy to be transferred from the County of London to the West Country. She's in her late fifties. I believe that she is exactly the right woman to have on the bench with you.'

Musgrove nodded. 'Very well, since you recommend her so strongly. What about the third?'

'Someone younger,' Francis replied. 'I thought of Brian Southern.'

Musgrove looked surprised. 'Some people,' he said after a pause, 'don't think a great deal of the Southern family. They're considered to be rather brash and pushy, if you know what I mean.'

'He's one of our newest and younger magistrates, aged thirty-eight and, as you probably know, chairman of a small engineering business in Stoneleigh Industrial Park.'

'He's a pretty sharp sort of fellow, I believe.'

'Perhaps, but the youth factor is, I consider, important. With you and him and Mrs Whitfield, I think we should have a well-balanced and representative bench, two men and one woman with as much a spread of different age groups as ever we could manage.'

Harold Musgrove finally acquiesced, and thus the composition of the bench to sit and hear the committal proceedings in the case of R. v. Ledbury had been settled and the hearing was fixed for Monday 22nd October.

On the day before the hearing when Mordecai was being driven west to the Royal Hunt Hotel, Francis Peyton made the long journey from Dorset to visit the home in Ealing where lived his wife Barbara who by now hardly recognized him and lived in a strange but not unhappy world of her own.

When the court had settled down, Francis Peyton rose and called on the case: 'Committal proceedings in the case of the Crown versus Mordecai Ledbury.'

Gwyn Vaughan rose to his feet, adjusted his spectacles and cleared his throat noisily, but before he could get out a word, Mordecai, still standing, said loudly, 'May it please you, sir. I am Mordecai Ledbury, the defendant, and represent myself, with the assistance of Mr Stapleton my solicitor seated here beside me. As is my right under the statute,' he went on, 'I apply for reporting restrictions on these proceedings to be lifted.'

There was a stir – and a gratified flurry in the crammed press box. This the reporters had not expected; they had believed that all they would be allowed to do would be to record but not to publish what was said in court. Colonel Musgrove looked down at Francis who rose and spoke to him. Gwyn Vaughan stood looking grave, his fingertips together, as though, Brian Southern thought, he was praying. In fact he was telling himself that if reporting restrictions were lifted that would be highly acceptable to him. Now the world, as well as the magistrates, would hear for the first time what had happened on 25th August in Water Meadow House – and from his lips.

'Since it is the wish of the accused,' the chairman said, 'reporting restrictions on these proceedings are now lifted.' He looked towards the press box. 'That'll please you chaps,' he said and smiled happily at the journalists, some of whom were already scrambling out of the press box making for the telephones to pass on the good news to their London offices. Above the noise of their exit Mordecai's voice went on.

'I hope, sir, that you will understand, as all the superior courts so graciously do, that my disability sometimes prevents me from speedily gaining my feet and I trust you will appreciate that should I have to intervene with any application at any time in the course of the proceedings, it is out of no discourtesy to the bench were I to do so from a seated position.' He collapsed with a clatter into his seat, laying his two sticks on the table in front of him.

Musgrove noted Mordecai's voice, the slight intonation of his long dead father, Aaron. A musical voice, Musgrove thought. Very interesting. Echoes of Syria? The Lebanon, perhaps? Certainly the Levant.

'Splendid,' he said, 'splendid. Well, let's get started.'

Elizabeth Fanshawe had been led by Henry's clerk to a seat reserved for her on the left of the court at right angles to the advocates' table. She had a clear view of Mordecai, his large head with the few strands of black hair pasted across the top, his skin the colour of parchment, his eyes closed. When she'd visited him his air of calm had not deceived her. She knew what he was feeling. She knew that he would not survive prison.

From his place on the bench, Brian Southern was also observing Mordecai. Ugly-looking fellow, he thought. But he had an air of authority about him. Perhaps this business might be interesting. He hadn't wanted to sit; he hadn't wanted to take the time away from his business. But Francis had persuaded him. Then Brian turned his attention to Gwyn Vaughan. Looks like an undertaker, he thought.

Vaughan began. 'I represent the Crown, and the accused as you have heard represents himself. I am asking that the accused be committed for trial at the assizes commencing in January next year on a charge of murder.

'The facts are as follows. On the night of Saturday 25th August of this year, or rather more probably in the early hours of the Sunday morning, the 26th, at Water

Meadow House, Kingsford Langley, a few miles from Dilminster, a young man, Stevie Rouse, was shot dead with a bullet through the back of his head. When the police came later in the morning–'

'Summoned by me,' growled Mordecai, his eyes still shut.

Vaughan paused and looked sternly at Mordecai. 'I was coming to that,' he said. 'The police had been summoned by the accused's driver. When they arrived shortly after noon at Water Meadow House, which is an isolated house, set in very neglected and overgrown grounds, they found the body of the young man. He was lying face down in the entrance to the main bedroom on the first floor, his head, or what remained of it, away from the bed and nearer to the open bedroom door. From the position of the body, it was clear to the police that the dead man–'

'Who had a poker in his hand,' again Mordecai growled.

Vaughan flung down his papers on the desk. 'I object to these interruptions.'

'Now, now, Mr Ledbury,' said the chairman with a surprising quickness. 'It doesn't help to have interruptions. We'll hear you later. Go on, Mr Vaughan.'

With an angry look at Mordecai, Vaughan continued. 'A poker was clasped in the dead man's right hand, but it was clear to the

206

police from the position of the corpse that the dead man had been shot in the back of his head as he was about to leave the bedroom. That Stevie Rouse had no right to be in the house, having broken in through a downstairs window, is certain, as it is equally certain that he had been shot from behind by a bullet from a .45 pistol fired by the accused. From what the accused later told the police, he was in bed when he became conscious that an intruder had entered his room and stretching out his hand he took up the pistol, for which no licence was held and which for some reason was lying on the top of the bedside table. He pointed it at Rouse and fired. The Crown say that the use of a pistol in those circumstances, namely the firing of such a deadly weapon at a man, who even if he was an intruder was at this time obviously leaving the room and was not threatening the accused and indeed had his back turned to the accused, was a wrongful act.' He paused and then went on. 'It was nothing less than the deliberate gunning down of another human being at a time when the accused was under no threat of attack and when no reasonable claim could be made that the accused was acting in self-defence. The pointing of the gun at Rouse, and the firing of it with sufficient accuracy to blow off Rouse's head, was deliberate. It was done with the clear intention of killing the man, or at the least of causing him grievous bodily harm; and in those circumstances it amounted to the crime of murder.'

Vaughan paused again. 'No one,' he continued, 'has the right to take the law into his or her own hands. This was nothing but an execution, the deliberate gunning down of another, which the law does not permit. If the law allowed any person to take up a firearm and shoot another who had come on to their land or into their premises, then as the magistrates will appreciate, any of the thousands of householders in the country-side who possess shotguns may believe that they were entitled to shoot any trespasser–'

There was a rumble. Mordecai was struggling to get to his feet.

'I object,' he said loudly. 'The duty of the representative of the Director of Public Prosecutions is to introduce the evidence so that you, sir, and your colleagues can decide, having heard the evidence in this case, whether or not there is a prima facie case to warrant me being sent to the assizes to stand trial. What a farmer may do with his twelve-bore shotgun in other circumstances in any other case is wholly immaterial. What you need to hear is the evidence in this case, and if the representative of the Director of Public Prosecutions wishes to make an opening address, he should stick to introducing to you the evidence he proposes to call in this case and this case only.'

And he subsided into his seat.

Francis rose from his place, turned and faced the bench. Colonel Musgrove bent towards him. The other two magistrates beside him leaned towards their chairman so that they could overhear the whispered conversation with the clerk. Francis resumed his seat and Colonel Musgrove cleared his throat.

'What you were saying, Mr Vaughan,' he began, 'was interesting but we have to get on so we feel you would help us most by coming to the evidence. We are anxious to hear what the witnesses have to tell us.'

Vaughan for a moment stood silent, breathing heavily. He had tried, he would tell the Director, but the court had stopped him.

'Very well,' he said at last and picked up the first of the witness statements. 'Then, I call the first witness. He is Police Officer Halliday who took photographs of the scene and has also prepared a plan of Water Meadow House which I hope will assist the bench when you hear the evidence of the later witnesses.'

Elizabeth was still watching Mordecai. He was leaning back in his chair, his eyes again closed. He did not open them when the police officer came to the witness box and produced the photographs and the plan of Water Meadow House. He did not even take

209

the photographs and the copy of the plan offered him by Vaughan. Henry leant across Mordecai and took them. The police officer went through the plan, indicating the details of the first-floor bedroom, the position of the dead body on the floor, and then the rooms on the ground floor, the library, the kitchen and the drawing room with the broken window. He next referred to the photographs, including those of the corpse. The booklet containing the photographs and the plan were marked Exhibit 1.

Mordecai rose to cross-examine. 'Look at your photograph of the corpse. Do you see some small, dark strips of material appearing underneath the remains of the head?'

Halliday examined the photograph. 'Yes, I do.'

'Could those pieces of dark material under the bloody remains of the deceased's head be the remains of a balaclava mask that the deceased was wearing at the time of his death?'

'I suppose they could.'

'Thank you. Now I don't see in your album any photograph of the surround of the door to the bedroom?'

'No, I didn't take any,' Halliday replied, surprised.

'Why not?'

Halliday paused. 'I did not think it was necessary.'

'Did you not consider it necessary to photograph the bullet hole in the surround to the door?'

Halliday looked bewildered. 'I did not see any bullet hole.'

'Did not the scene-of-crime officer point it out to you?'

'No, he did not.'

'Did not Detective Sergeant West or Chief Superintendent Blake?'

'No.'

'So none of these police officers ever showed you the bullet mark in the surround of the door?'

'No.'

Mordecai stood silent, slowly shaking his head. 'How odd,' he said as he once more resumed his seat.

Halliday's evidence, which had been taken down by the stenographer directly on to her machine, was then read back to him. He signed it and left the box. This procedure was followed at the end of each witness's evidence.

Next in the box came the police surgeon who conducted the post-mortem and certified that the deceased, Stevie Rouse, had died of a massive gunshot wound to the back of his head, time of death the early hours of Sunday 26th August. He produced the bullet, which was marked Exhibit 2. In cross-examination Mordecai asked him,

'Did you note the contents of the dead man's stomach?'

'I did.'

'What did you find?'

'Evidence that shortly before he was killed he had been drinking heavily.'

This witness was followed by Leslie Barnes, the firearm expert. Vaughan produced the pistol, which was marked Exhibit 3. Barnes told the court that it was of American manufacture, made some eighty years ago in the late nineteenth century. It was of .45 calibre, issued at the time, he believed, to the United States army. 'Although of such ancient manufacture, it is a fine piece,' he said. He was handling it lovingly, balancing it in his hand. 'It had been well maintained, kept clean and oiled and in perfect working order.'

Mordecai once more heaved himself slowly to his feet. 'When were you first asked to inspect this weapon?'

The witness looked at his notes. 'On 31st August last,' he replied.

'Was it clear to you from your examination of the barrel and the chamber that two shots had recently been fired from the pistol?'

'It was. There were two used cartridges in the chamber.'

Mordecai paused. 'Two spent cartridges, two bullets fired,' he said, Then he asked. 'Is the weapon now unloaded?'

'It is.'

'Will you please press the trigger?' The witness did as he was asked, holding the pistol above his head so that the barrel pointed to the ceiling. The sound of the hammer striking the empty chamber could be easily heard in the silent court.

'Again, please.'

The click was repeated.

'Now press the trigger and keep your finger on it.' The chamber circled. At the second click, Mordecai cried suddenly, 'Stop.' Then he went on, 'Does it require much pressure on the trigger to fire the weapon?'

'No, it responds to quite light pressure.'

'And despite its age, the action operates perfectly smoothly?'

'It does. As I said, it has been excellently maintained.'

'So it does not require much pressure on the trigger to fire that pistol, and if the finger is kept on the trigger it will continue to fire as the chamber revolves, bringing round a fresh bullet for firing. Is that correct?'

'It is.'

'Thank you. That is all.' Then, almost as an afterthought, he added, 'Perhaps the bench may care to examine the pistol for themselves?'

The pistol was taken from the witness by the usher and handed to Colonel Musgrove. He broke the pistol expertly, examined the firing mechanism and the chamber, snapped it shut and pressed the trigger, twice. Then he handed it to Mrs Whitfield and after her to Brian Southern. The stenographer read what she had recorded and Leslie Barnes signed the deposition and left the box.

'I call next Detective Sergeant West.'

West took the oath in a practised, professional manner. In answering Vaughan he referred to his notebook and spoke slowly, leaving plenty of time for the stenographer to record his answers on her machine. He began by describing his arrival at Water Meadow House with Chief Superintendent Thomas Blake on Sunday 26th August. He told the court that the house had been the family home of a Major Roderick Fairbairn, a much mutilated war hero who had lived there as a recluse since his return from the war twenty-six years ago and had died in the house earlier this year. He went on to say that he learnt subsequently that Major Fairbairn had bequeathed the house and its contents to his first cousin, Mr Mordecai Ledbury, the accused. Mr Stapleton was the executor of Major Fairbairn's will.

'The house had obviously been greatly neglected over many years,' he said, 'and was in a very dilapidated condition.'

He then described how on arrival they found the accused sitting in the hall flanked by his solicitor, Mr Henry Stapleton, and his driver. The accused told them that he had spent the night alone in the house examining the family documents, many of which were in boxes in the library, and that in the small hours of the morning he had woken to find that a man had come into his bedroom. 'The accused told us,' West went on, 'that upstairs we would find the body of the man whom he, the accused, had shot with a pistol he had found in the bedroom. The accused then indicated a pistol that was on the table behind him.'

Vaughan handed him the pistol, Exhibit 3, which West identified as the pistol that the accused said he had used. The accused, West continued, had said that the pistol had been lying on the table beside his bed when he was woken by the intruder. Later the police discovered that the body was that of a young man called Stevie Rouse.

West went on to say that he had examined the whole of the house, finding a broken window in the drawing room and in the kitchen the remnants of what seemed like a picnic and three empty bottles of champagne.

Colonel Musgrove interrupted. 'How many bottles, did you say?'

'Three, sir. Mr Stapleton told us that he had shared one with the accused earlier on the Saturday at lunchtime. The other two the accused admitted he had drunk the evening before, the Saturday evening.'

Musgrove looked round the court,

apparently smiling.

West then described his arrival with Chief Superintendent Blake at Albany in London with a warrant to arrest the accused on a charge of murder.

'What did the accused say when you arrested him?' asked Vaughan.

West referred to his note. 'The accused said that he would make a statement, which I wrote down. He then signed it and handed it to us.'

'Is this the statement the accused handed to you?' Vaughan asked, as he handed a document to the usher who took it to the witness.

West examined it and said that it was.

'May the document please be marked Exhibit 4.'

When this had been done, Vaughan said, 'Will you please read the statement to the court.'

West did so and then handed it to the usher.

'Remain there, please,' said Vaughan and sat down. Mordecai got slowly to his feet.

'On the journey in the car to Water Meadow House on the morning of Sunday 26th August, did you and Chief Superintendent Blake have any conversation about me?'

'Just that it was you whom we expected to see at the house when we got there.'

'Was that all?'

'Yes.'

'Was anything said about a conference held shortly before this time by the Chief Constable, when the Chief Constable had complained about me?'

'It may have been mentioned.'

'Anything may have been mentioned but *was* it mentioned that the Chief Constable had been complaining about the behaviour of members of the bar defending in criminal cases who made allegations about the integrity of the police and in particular referred to me?'

Before West could reply Vaughan rose. 'I object to this line of questioning. It has no relevance to the facts surrounding the killing of Stevie Rouse.'

'It may not but it goes to credit, the credit of this police officer,' Mordecai said savagely.

'But I understood,' went on Vaughan, 'that none of the facts spoken to by this officer is challenged. So what is the relevance of all this?'

'The relevance is this. What lies behind this prosecution is spite and–'

Vaughan was not to be deterred. Francis was on his feet whispering to the chairman as Vaughan said, 'This prosecution is founded upon the facts that the witnesses speak to. If those facts are sufficient to persuade the court that they amount to a prima facie case against the accused, then

217

he should be committed for trial. That's all there is to it. Allegations of spite have nothing to do with it.'

'The court should be aware,' thundered Mordecai, 'of the circumstances behind the case.'

'Mr Ledbury,' said Henry Musgrove. Francis had resumed his seat. 'The bench would like you to stick to the facts and make any challenge you wish to what the officer says about those facts.'

Mordecai stood silent, breathing heavily. Vaughan from his seat smirked and nodded vigorously. Henry put out his hand as though to restrain Mordecai who brushed it aside. For some moments he stood still and silent. At last, he shook his head and said, 'Very well.' He turned to West in the witness box. 'In the car to the house, did you talk about me?'

'I think it was said that it was funny to be going to interview you about a shooting in the house.'

'And was this a source of considerable satisfaction to you, that you were on your way to investigate a shooting with which I was concerned?'

'It was a little – ironic.'

'Very well, ironic. Because now you were about to question me about a shooting?'

'Yes.'

'That being in your minds when you

arrived, Chief Superintendent Blake was not exactly friendly when he came into the house to interview me, was he?'

'I don't know what you mean by friendly. He was perfectly correct.'

'Was he? He thought, did he not, that this was an opportunity to get his own back on someone he'd been told by the Chief Constable was not very friendly to the police, didn't he?'

'Mr Blake was doing his duty.'

'Let us examine the situation with which you were confronted when you came to Water Meadow House. The dead man was a burglar. He had broken into the house, which had no telephone. He had entered a bedroom of a cripple, armed with a poker in the middle of the night and, as you checked, the electric light throughout the house had fused. You did discover that, did you not?'

'Yes, we found that at some time all the lights had fused. We couldn't say when.'

'What do you mean by that? Do you doubt that the lights had fused in the middle of the night?'

'No, but as I said we couldn't say when they had fused.'

'But I had told you that the lights had fused before I had gone to sleep, before the burglar had broken into the house. Did you believe that?'

'We couldn't tell when the lights had

fused,' West repeated.

'Of course you could not. I ask you again. Did you believe me when I told you that the lights had fused before the burglar broke into the house?'

'It wasn't a matter of believing you or not but–'

'But you were so pleased to have me to question that you didn't accept anything that I told you?'

'We did believe you when you said that you had shot the man.'

'Oh, yes, you believed that. You believed that Mordecai Ledbury had shot a man and you were delighted to have the opportunity to investigate the matter?'

'We were doing our duty.'

'A duty that you and Mr Blake found particularly agreeable. Is that not right?'

'As I said, it was ironic, you being the person that was concerned.'

'And if you could pin a crime on Mordecai Ledbury you would be delighted, is that not right?'

'I said, we were doing our duty.'

'Tell me now about Steven Rouse. He was known to the police as a petty criminal, but known to associate with more serious criminals, was he not?'

'We only discovered who the dead man was later. And, yes, he was as you describe him.'

'Now I want to ask you about the pistol,

Exhibit 3. But first, did you remove from the library of that house certain manuscripts written, it appeared, by Major Fairbairn?'

'I did.'

'Subsequently did you read those manuscripts?'

'I did.'

'Have you them in court?'

'Mr Vaughan has them.'

Mordecai turned to Vaughan and held out his hand. Vaughan delved into his black briefcase and brought out a file. He handed it to Mordecai who leafed through the manuscripts. He extracted one from the file and handed it to the usher. 'Do you identify this as one of the manuscripts that you read and does it refer to Major Fairbairn's acquisition of a pistol in 1940 and his keeping it in the drawer of the table by his bed?'

West looked at the manuscript. 'Yes,' he said. 'That is correct.'

'May this be marked Exhibit 5?'

Mordecai went on. 'So from your reading of the writings of Major Fairbairn, you learnt that this pistol Exhibit 3 had belonged to him, that he had acquired it during the war and that he had kept it in the bedside table in the bedroom in which he slept?'

'It so appears from what Major Fairbairn had written.'

'The court has heard that the pistol had been carefully maintained and was in

221

excellent working order. You are not suggesting, are you, that it was I who had cleaned and oiled it and kept in good working order?'

'I don't know who had kept it maintained–'

'Are you suggesting that it was I?'

West hesitated. 'I can only say that I don't know anything about the pistol.'

'Do you seriously tell the court that you thought it might have been me who maintained it?'

'No, I can't exactly say that. All I know is that it was reported to be in good working order and had been recently fired.'

'You read from what Major Fairbairn wrote that he, who had suffered devastating war wounds and the loss in an air raid of the woman he was to have married, had kept the pistol by him and had on occasions contemplated taking his own life. It was *he* who must have maintained it, was it not?'

'It seems so from the writings.'

'Very well then, and that was the pistol that was fired on the night of Saturday 25th August, was it not?'

'Yes.'

'And how many times was that pistol fired during that night?'

'Twice.'

'One bullet, Exhibit 2, the bullet taken from the dead man's skull, had struck the man's head and killed him. What about the other?'

'There was a bullet hole in the surround of the bedroom door.'

'And the bullet was lodged in that surround, was it not?'

'I believe so.'

'Did you see it there, lodged in the wood?'

'I did.'

'Where is that bullet?'

'The scene-of-crime officer, I believe, removed it and–'

'I asked where is that bullet?'

'I don't know.'

'You don't know!'

'I know it was removed from where it was lodged in the door surround by, I believe, the scene-of-crime officer.'

'Who, presumably, placed it in a polythene bag with the other items that were removed from the house?'

'Yes.'

'I repeat. Where is that bullet?'

West shifted uneasily in the witness box. 'It seems to have been mislaid,' he said lamely.

'Mislaid! A bullet from the pistol that had killed a man, a burglar, has been mislaid? Is that what you are telling the court?'

'It's very unfortunate but it's gone missing. The bullet cannot now be found and–'

'Unfortunate! It's more than unfortunate. It is scandalous! A prime exhibit that had been taken into the possession of the police has gone missing, and cannot now be found! Is that what you are telling the court?'

'Yes. But I know it existed. I saw it. And it wasn't the bullet that killed Stevie Rouse.'

'We know that. There were two shots fired that night. One hit the door surround; the other hit the back of the burglar's head, killing him instantaneously.' Mordecai paused. 'Is it not consistent with the facts that the first shot hit the surround to the door and was fired when the burglar was standing at the foot of the bed and the second shot, the shot that killed him, was fired when he had turned away? Isn't that consistent with what you discovered?'

'I suppose it is. We don't know.'

'No, you don't know. But isn't that consistent with what could have happened that night and wholly consistent with what was expressed in my statement Exhibit 4?'

'It's possible.'

'Bring me Exhibit 3,' Mordecai said to the usher. The usher brought the pistol to Mordecai who laid it on the table beside him. 'Now follow me, please, officer. My statement claims that suddenly being woken, I stretched out my hand for the torch.' Mordecai, still looking at the witness and not at the pistol, stretched out his hand and picked up the pistol. 'Instead of falling on to the torch, my hand fell on to the pistol and, raising it, I fired it in order to scare off

224

the burglar who was armed with what we now know was a poker.' Mordecai was pointing the pistol in the direction of the witness box. He pulled the trigger. 'The first shot struck the door surround, the burglar then swung around.' Mordecai pressed the trigger again. 'The second shot struck him.'

Mordecai laid down the pistol. For a time there was silence in the court. Then Mordecai said very quietly, 'Isn't that consistent with what I told you and with the evidence of where the bullets lodged?'

West again hesitated. 'It could be, yes.'

Mordecai sat down. It took some time for the evidence to be read back to West who then signed it.

'Time for lunch,' Musgrove said jovially. He looked round the court. 'We'll be back at two o'clock. See you all then.'

The chairs scraped back, the magistrates disappeared and the court broke into a buzz of noise.

2

Webster and Elizabeth had taken over the advocates' robing room for lunch. There seemed to be nowhere else in the courthouse and no one stopped them so they laid on the table sandwiches and a flask of coffee. Webster produced Mordecai's travelling carrier that held two half-bottles of champagne. Mordecai, followed by Henry, came in and sank into a chair.

'How are we doing?' he asked Elizabeth.

She saw that he needed reassurance and squeezed his hand. 'Good,' she said, with a confidence she did not feel.

Webster was opening the wine when Gwyn Vaughan came through the door. He pulled up, astonished by the sound of the popping cork.

'What's the meaning of this?' he said.

'We've commandeered the room for our lunch,' Mordecai growled. 'There's nowhere else.'

'And where pray do you imagine that I am to be?'

'Go to the pub.'

Henry, who had joined them, put a hand on Mordecai's shoulder to restrain him.

'Mr Ledbury can't easily get across the street to the Castle Hotel and be back in time, and there's nowhere else.'

'You might have asked,' said Vaughan. He took his raincoat from the peg, looking distastefully at the wine. 'I shall get some coffee from across the road.' He made to leave. At the door he picked up his briefcase.

'You're right to keep a hand on that,' said Mordecai, 'or we might learn some more about the Director's tricks.'

Vaughan said coldly, 'There's only one

more witness, the Superintendent,' and he turned on his heel.

Webster filled one of the tumblers with champagne. Signalling to him, Mordecai said, 'I want you to slip across to the hotel and see who's talking to whom.'

Webster looked up surprised. Mordecai went on, 'The last witness. If you don't find him in the Castle, take a look in any of the nearby public houses.'

'Right,' said Webster, moving towards the door.

'Be back at five minutes to two to report,' Mordecai called after him.

The telephone on a ledge in the corner of the room rang. Henry picked up the receiver. After listening for a moment, he said, 'One moment please,' and covered the receiver with his hand. 'It's the Director of Public Prosecutions. He wants to speak to Vaughan.'

Mordecai heaved himself from his chair, stumbled across the room and took the telephone from Henry. 'Vaughan's not here. If you want to know how the case is going, Threadgold, I can tell you that the police are lying like troopers.' He put down the receiver and went back to his chair.

In the judge's room the magistrates were also eating sandwiches and Francis Peyton moved around pouring coffee.

'I saw the Lord Lieutenant's wife in court,' said the Colonel.

'I believe she's a great friend of Mr Ledbury,' said Francis.

'Friends in high places,' said Southern.

'I suppose she's interested in the case as are many others,' went on Francis. 'It is certainly a very unusual case.' He paused in the pouring of the coffee. 'Very unusual.'

'Fancy the police losing that bullet,' said Southern.

'How many more witnesses?' asked Musgrove.

'Only one, Colonel,' Francis replied. 'The Chief Superintendent.'

'Then what happens?'

'There'll be a submission, I imagine, by the defence,' said Francis. 'That will come at the end of the evidence. Then you retire and decide.'

Mrs Whitfield rose from her chair. 'I should like to wash and brush-up.'

'Let me show you,' said Francis. He led her down the corridor. 'On the left,' he said.

Mrs Whitfield laid a hand on his arm. 'When did you last see dear Barbara?'

'Yesterday.'

'How was she?'

'The same.'

'Does she still recognize you?'

'I'm not sure. I only visit once a month now. It's too painful. This is the bathroom.' Francis opened the door for her.

He returned to the judge's room. 'What

did you make of the weapon, Chairman?' Brian Southern was asking.

'A museum piece, as the man said, but in very good order.'

'Easy to fire?'

'Oh, yes, very. Not much pressure needed on the trigger. So Fairbairn got it in the war. It's a very powerful weapon. It made a pretty good mess of Rouse's head.' He was thinking of the photographs.

'Fairbairn wrote a lot about it,' said Francis. 'It's in Exhibit 5. I took the liberty of taking it from the court in case you wished to have a look at it during the adjournment.'

'Good idea. Pull up a chair, Southern,' Colonel Musgrove said.

Francis handed him the file. 'I've tagged where he wrote about the gun.'

Mrs Whitfield returned. Francis offered her a sandwich. She took one and looked up to him with a smile. 'How long do we expect to be this afternoon?'

'There's only one more witness, the Chief Superintendent.'

Southern said, 'I suppose he'll say the same as the Detective Sergeant.'

'The witnesses who have already given evidence are not allowed to talk to anyone who is yet to give evidence,' said Francis gently. 'There's a very strict rule about that. And after him, as I have just told the chairman, I expect there will be a submission by the defence that the prosecution has failed to make out a prima facie case for murder. After that you retire to make your decision – whether to send the accused to stand trial for murder at the assizes or...' He paused again. 'Or decline to commit the accused and discharge him.' He turned to take the coffee cups to the table. 'Is there anything further I can get you, Chairman?'

'No,' said the Colonel. He took out his hunter watch from his waistcoat pocket. 'We'll come in at two o'clock precisely.'

Chief Superintendent William Blake, in a smart blue suit and dark blue tie, was even more practised and fluent than West in the technique of testifying. In reply to Vaughan, he went over the ground that had been covered by West before the adjournment: the police's arrival at the house, what had been said, what they had found, and later the arrest at Albany. He had been giving evidence for a little over twenty minutes before Mordecai rose to cross-examine. When he was finally on his feet, he stood silent for several seconds, staring at the witness. Blake looked fixedly to his front, away from Mordecai. Then the cross-examination began.

'Where did you have your lunch today, Mr Blake?'

The question surprised the witness. He turned to face Mordecai. Two red spots appeared high on his cheekbones.

'Lunch? Today?'

'Yes. Did I not make myself clear?'

'I – I went to a public house, around the corner, here in the town.'

'Not to the Castle?'

'No. It, I think, is called the Rose.'

'Why not the Castle? It is nearer and it's where most people from the court go for lunch.'

'I preferred the Rose.'

'Away from people who had been in court?'

'That was not particularly the reason. The Rose is quieter.'

'But the Rose is some way from the court, is it not?'

'A little way, not much.'

'And when you got to the Rose, did you go to the snug?'

Blake hesitated, looked at Mordecai and then resumed staring in front of him towards the bench. 'I was in the snug, yes,' he said at last.

'Alone?'

Blake paused. 'No, I had a companion.'

Mordecai turned to the back of the court and called out, 'Mr Webster, will you please come forward and step near to the witness box?'

Webster came from behind the dock and stood in full view of the witness box and the bench. Mordecai said to Blake, 'Did you notice this gentleman when you were lunching in the snug at the Rose public house?'

Blake turned to look at Webster. 'I can't say I did.'

'Did he not look into the snug where you and your companion were sitting?'

'He may have.' Blake looked at Mordecai. 'I don't see what this has to do with the evidence I've come to give.'

'Can't you? It might have much to do with your evidence, particularly when you answer my next question. Which is: who was your companion at lunch?'

Blake hesitated. The red spots were even more noticeable on his face. He was looking again at the bench, away from Mordecai.

'Answer, please,' said Mordecai.

Blake looked again at Webster and then at Mordecai, then straight ahead of him before he said almost in a mumble, 'Detective Sergeant West.'

'The officer who had just given evidence. Did you think that was a proper thing to do?'

'We didn't speak about the case if that's what you're suggesting,' said Blake.

'You didn't speak about the case in which Sergeant West had just given evidence? Not a single word throughout the hour you spent together while you – let me see.' He looked down at the paper he was holding. 'While you were drinking half a pint of beer with your sandwich and your companion – let me see, yes, your companion was having a tot of whisky. Did Sergeant West explain why he needed whisky after giving his evidence?'

'I told you we didn't speak about the case.'

'So you have said – or rather, so you have just sworn – on oath. Sworn that you didn't speak at all with Sergeant West about the case in which you knew you were about to testify? Is that what you ask the magistrates to believe?'

'It is.'

'Mr Blake, you are an experienced police officer. You have participated in many trials. You know the rules. You knew that you were a witness about to give evidence. You knew that Sergeant West had just given his. What were you doing lunching in company with the witness who had just given evidence?'

'We came from Stoneleigh together in the car this morning. It was just lunch. As I said, we didn't mention the case.'

'You didn't lunch at the Castle, the hotel opposite the court where most people from the court go to lunch. Instead you chose another public house around the corner and went into the snug, which has room only for two. A discreet and private place to be together. Were you trying to hide the fact that you and West were lunching together?'

'Certainly not. I saw no harm in it.'

'Didn't you? The two police officers in the

case, one of whom had given his evidence and been cross-examined, the other about to give evidence and be cross-examined. The two police witnesses in the case, talking together, putting their heads together. Wasn't that what it must have looked like if – I repeat - if you happened to be observed? And you say you saw no harm in that?'

'No, I did not.'

'No harm in it?'

'No.'

'Is that standard form in your force? To behave like that?'

'As I have said, we didn't talk about the case.'

'So you have sworn. And that is what you want the magistrates to believe.'

'It is the truth.'

'Well, I suggest you spoke a great deal about the case when you were with Sergeant West?'

'I told you. We did not.'

Mordecai kept silent, looking at Blake who kept his face fixed to his front. The silence lasted for quite a time. Vaughan thought of intervening; he half rose and then sat back. Stupid police, he thought. At last Mordecai turned from facing the witness and moved a little behind the table. Then he swung back to face Blake and barked:

'You are the officer in charge of this case. When you were at Water Meadow House on the morning of Sunday 26th August did you see the bullet that was lodged in the wooden surround to the bedroom door?'

'I did.'

'The magistrates have been told that it is missing. How could it have gone missing?'

'I cannot tell. It was recorded as coming into police possession.'

'Doesn't that show extraordinary incompetence by the force in which you are a senior officer?'

'If you say so.'

'I say so! Shouldn't everyone say so?'

'Perhaps.'

'And you can give the magistrates no explanation of why it cannot be produced?'

'No. I cannot. But I don't see why the production of that bullet is so important. We know two shots were fired.'

Mordecai paused again. 'Returning to your lunch with West, was the missing bullet mentioned?'

'No, it was not.'

'Was my name mentioned?'

'No.'

'So what were you talking about?'

Blake hesitated again. 'General things, family things.'

'But not a word about this case, not a word about this court, not a word about me? Of course, my name had been mentioned, had it not, when you and West were being driven

235

to Water Meadow House on the morning of Sunday 26th August?'

'Yes. We knew that you would be at the house when we got there.'

'And your duty that morning was not altogether displeasing to you, was it?'

'I had my duty to do.'

'Which, I may remind you, ought also to have included making certain that none of the exhibits went missing?'

'I have explained,' Blake replied angrily. 'The mislaying of the bullet was most unfortunate.'

'When you had assembled all the facts and collected all the exhibits, or thought you had, and taken all the statements, did you then compile a report?'

'I did.'

'And did you present your report to the Director of Public Prosecutions?'

'Yes.'

'Were you and the Chief Constable pleased when you learnt that the DPP had decided to prosecute Mordecai Ledbury?'

'I can't speak for the Chief but as far as I was concerned, I was satisfied that what had been done and what was going to be done was as a result of my executing my duty.'

'An agreeable duty?'

'My duty.'

'Tell me, when you saw the DPP, did he say anything about me?'

'Of course your name was mentioned. The whole conference was about the shooting of Rouse by you.'

After a pause Mordecai went on, 'Now let us turn to the man who was shot having broken into the house, Stevie Rouse. It must have been quite a trial to you having him on your patch, as it is sometimes called?'

'He was a troublesome lad.'

'Had Rouse been involved in any violence prior to 25th August of this year?'

'He'd been involved in some minor cases of assault, nothing serious.'

'Had there been much housebreaking in the neighbourhood prior to 25th August of this year?'

'A fair amount.'

'In early July was Rouse suspected of having tried to gain admittance to a house in the Stoneleigh Vale Estate in June and been frightened off by a man, the householder?'

'He was one of a number of suspects.'

'On 31st July did another householder, an elderly woman, a widow who lived alone, report that a man had broken into her bungalow in Nightingale Lane in Stoneleigh and robbed her of £300 of her savings?'

'Yes, there was a report of such an incident.'

'Was that intruder ever caught?'

'No.'

'Did the elderly woman suffer considerable

237

trauma as a result of waking and discovering the intruder in her bungalow?'

'Naturally. She was very frightened. The man was wearing some kind of dark, woolly mask over his face.'

'Look, please, at the photographs, Exhibit 1.'The usher brought the booklet to the witness. 'Look at the picture of the dead man. Can you see small strips of material under what remains of his head?'

Blake examined the photograph. 'I can make out something dark.'

'In the opinion of the officer who took that photograph those strips of dark material could have been the remains of the balaclava helmet that the dead man was wearing when he was shot.'

Blake put the photo aside. 'It could be. I can't be sure.'

'You remember, do you not, that in my statement, Exhibit 4, I said that when I woke and saw the figure at the end of the bed, he was wearing a balaclava helmet?'

'You said that, yes.'

'And I said that the man was holding something in his hand which later turned out to be a poker?'

'You did.'

'Did you test the poker for fingerprints?'

'We did, yes.'

'And whose fingerprints did you find on the poker?'

'Rouse's.'

'Anyone else's?'

'No.'

'At the time of his death Rouse was holding a torch?'

'Yes. That was found near the body.'

Mordecai, breathing heavily, stared at him. Then he picked up a piece of paper from the pile in front of him. 'Very well, Superintendent,' he said at last, 'let us return to the incident when the elderly lady in Nightingale Lane had woken to find a man in her bungalow. You have told us that she said the man had a dark, woolly mask over his face?'

'She did.'

'Did she also say that the intruder was armed?'

'She thought the man had a stick or a bludgeon.'

'What consequence was suffered by her as a result of her experience?'

'She was hospitalized. Later she moved away from the district.'

'Was Rouse suspected of having committed that crime?'

'He was again one of the suspects. Nothing could be proved.'

Mordecai paused. Then he said very quietly, 'Rouse, whom I shot, was one of the suspects in July when a householder surprised a man trying to gain entry to his house; he was again one of the suspects

239

when on 31st July an elderly woman woke to discover a man in her house. And at the end of August, Rouse was found dead in Water Meadow House, his hand clenching a poker' – Mordecai emphasized the words – 'and with the remains of a mask beneath his body. Is that not so?'

'Yes.'

Mordecai paused. 'That is all,' he began and then said, 'No, there is one other matter.' He turned to Henry who handed him a folded newspaper. 'Will you take a look at that, please?'

The usher brought the folded newspaper to the witness.

'Is that a copy of the *London Evening Echo?*'

Blake examined it. 'It appears so,' he said.

'What is the date of that edition of that London evening newspaper?'

'11th September this year.'

'Is there a photograph on the front page of that edition of 11th September?'

Blake paused. The red spots had re-appeared on his cheekbones. 'There is,' he said.

'It is, is it not, a picture of a police car in the forecourt of what I suggest is Albany off Piccadilly in London?'

'Could be.'

'And does the photograph show me sitting in the back of that police car next to you?'

'It seems so.'

'Now let me remind you. It was on 11th September at eight o'clock in the morning that you came to my home in Albany to arrest me. Isn't that correct?'

'I think that is the date, yes.'

'And by some extraordinary chance on that very morning there happened to be a press photographer in the courtyard of Albany ready and able to take a photograph of the famous QC just after the famous Superintendent had arrested him.' Mordecai paused. 'How do you think that came about?'

'I can't speak for the actions of the press.'

'Can't you? Perhaps not all of their actions but of this one, I suggest, you can. For who else knew that on 11th September you would be coming to arrest me?'

Blake paused. 'The Chief Constable?' Mordecai asked.

Blake shifted awkwardly in the witness box. 'He'd know. There are others too in the HQ, clerks, telephonists, they might know.'

'Are you suggesting one of them might have alerted the press?'

'Could be. I don't know.'

'Don't you? Do you really suggest that one of the clerks without prompting and without your knowledge or approval took it into his head and telephoned the *London Evening Echo* and told them to be at Albany at 8 a.m. on 11th September and they'd get an interesting picture? Are you suggesting a

241

clerk did that as I said, without prompting?'

'I can't say,' muttered Blake.

'No, you can't say that, can you? So who really alerted the press that you were going to make an arrest at 8 a.m. on 11th September?'

Blake was silent. 'It was not me, was it,' said Mordecai quietly, 'for I did not know that you were coming and I would hardly have sought publicity for the occasion. So I ask again. Who alerted the police that the energetic, efficient Chief Superintendent from the West Country was about to make the sensational arrest of the dangerous criminal who lived in Albany off Piccadilly on the morning of 11th September?'

Vaughan jumped to his feet. 'What has this to do with the killing of Rouse? This is quite irrelevant. I object to the introduction of this. If the accused has any objection to what happened in the course of his arrest he should raise it with the proper authorities. It has nothing to do with whether or not the prosecution has shown there is a prima facie case for committal for trial.'

Before the chairman could reply, Mordecai said quietly, 'Strictly perhaps not, but the magistrates may think that it has to do with the whole conduct of this prosecution.' He subsided into his chair, one of his sticks falling to the floor with a crash.

Vaughan, who had remained standing, said to Blake, 'Was the decision to prosecute

242

a matter for you or was it solely a matter for the Director of Public Prosecutions?'

'The Director took the decision, no one else.'

'That is all. Thank you.'

The evidence was read back to the Superintendent. When Blake had signed his statement of evidence, Vaughan addressed the bench:

'That is the evidence, sir–'

Mordecai, speaking from where he sat, interrupted. 'Not all the evidence. The prosecution has not considered it worthwhile calling Ronald Taylor. I think they should.'

Vaughan looked down at Mordecai, bewildered. 'Taylor?' he began. 'Taylor? Who is Taylor?'

Mordecai was struggling to his feet. 'Ronald Taylor was a friend of Stevie Rouse and was with him for part of the night on which Rouse died. The police have interviewed him.' Henry handed Mordecai a paper. 'I have a statement from him.'

Vaughan turned and signalled furiously to Blake who came and whispered to him. Francis Peyton was on his feet speaking to the magistrates.

After listening to Francis, Colonel Musgrove said, 'Mr Vaughan, who is this man Mr Ledbury is talking about? If he has anything important to say, shouldn't we hear him?'

Blake was still whispering in Vaughan's

ear. Vaughan straightened and said, 'One moment, sir, if you please.' The whispering restarted. Eventually Blake backed away. Vaughan said, 'The police did interview Ronald Taylor but they decided that Mr Taylor could not add anything material to the evidence because, of course, he was not present when Rouse was killed. It was not felt that Mr Taylor could realistically assist the court and for this reason it was not proposed to call him as a witness. In any event Mr Taylor is not here, and–'

'Oh, yes he is,' said Mordecai. 'He is outside.' He turned and called out, 'Bring him in, Webster.'

'Will someone tell me what's going on?' said Colonel Musgrove genially.

'A new witness, sir,' said Mordecai. 'I think you should hear what he has to say.'

Francis turned and once more spoke to the bench. Then Musgrove said, 'Well, if it is relevant we'll hear what he has to say but as Mr Vaughan has pointed out, he can't have witnessed the shooting.'

There was a commotion at the back of the court, the swing doors opened and Webster appeared, preceded by a young man with long sandy hair who looked about him with an embarrassed grin on his face. Webster motioned to the youth to go nearer to the bench.

'Are you Mr Taylor?' Musgrove asked him.

'That's right,' the young man said, now grinning more broadly. 'Ron Taylor, that's me.'

Again Francis Peyton rose and spoke to the magistrates. Then Musgrove asked, 'Mr Ledbury, do you want us to hear what Mr Taylor has to say?'

'I do, sir.'

'Very well, we'll hear him. You can call him as your witness.'

'But–' began Vaughan.

'No, Mr Vaughan,' Musgrove replied firmly, 'you didn't think Mr Taylor could help us so let Mr Ledbury call him and we can judge if his evidence helps us or not.'

The usher led Taylor to the witness box and administered the oath. By then the grin had disappeared and he looked about him nervously.

'Is your name Ron Taylor,' Mordecai asked, 'and do you live at 6 Windsor Gardens, Russell Road, Stoneleigh?'

'That's right.'

'Did you know the deceased, Steven Rouse?'

'Stevie Rouse? Of course I knew him. We were kids together, weren't we?'

'When did you last see him?'

'Well, he's dead, isn't he? I saw him the night he was killed, shot he was, wasn't he, in the old house. At least that's what they say.'

'Do you mean Water Meadow House?'

'Yes, that's what it's called, isn't it?'

'Do you know that house?'

'Of course I do. The old man with the beard used to live there. When we was kids we used to creep through the grass and the shrubbery and watch him. He made us laugh and when he'd hear us he'd come and chase us and we'd run away, didn't we?'

'Have you ever been inside that house?'

Taylor shifted his feet in the witness box, looking around him. 'No. We went there again years after, wasn't it, when we were growed and Stevie came back from Bridport where he'd gone with his Dad and Ma. We thought the old place was a ruin and empty and we went to take a look at it one night after Stevie and I had been down in the pub. I didn't go inside but Stevie did and then all of a sudden he came out running, scared like, and we ran off, didn't we?'

'Was that the night that the owner, the old Major Fairbairn died?'

'I heard so after. That was what had scared Stevie, hadn't it?'

'Did you go on seeing Stevie after that night?'

'He was with his family in Bridport, see. He came back one night later—'

'How much later?'

'I don't know, do I? Some weeks, I expect. I met him in the pub, just by chance. He was there before me. Quite a surprise it was.

He'd been drinking–'

'What was he drinking?'

'Rum and light ale, wasn't it? Something like that. He'd had a skinful when I came in. He had quite a bit of cash with him.'

'Did he have more to drink while you were with him?'

'Of course he did. A lot more.'

'Did he then tell you what he had in mind?'

'He said he was going back to the old place. He said he thought there was a lot there he wanted to get his hands on. Last time, I said, you ran away scared but he said he wouldn't run again. If there was anyone there, he'd deal with them.'

'What did you think he meant by deal with them?'

'Thump them. I don't know.'

'What do you mean by thump them?'

'Hit them. He wasn't going to be scared off this time, see. That's what he said. He said this time he was going to get what he'd come for.'

'What was that?'

'Things in the house. Silver, he said, money. The old man, he said, was a miser. Then he said that anyhow the place was empty now. I said don't be daft, you've had too much to drink. He asked me to go with him. I said no, but he went on about it, saying again he wasn't going to run this time. So then he said come on, help me to get there, keep a lookout, see. I'm just going to have a look around. I said you're drunk. It'll be a lark, he said, we'll go there like we did when we was kids.'

'Did he say anything more about whether anyone was there?'

'He said no one was there but if there was he'd thump anyone who was. He said the house was empty, it's a ruin. The old man's dead. Well, he took the car, see, and started to drive. I said again you're too drunk but we got to a place under the trees and he started to drink again, rum from a small bottle. There was moonlight. Then he said I'm off. I had to help him through the bushes. He was falling all over the place. I said I'm not coming in with you and he said please yourself and he went to the house and I saw him go through a window.'

'How did he get through the window?'

'Smashed the glass, didn't he? Made quite a noise he did.'

'What happened then?'

'I just waited, behind a tree on the other side of some bushes.'

'For how long did you wait?'

'I don't know, do I? Quite a time. Then I heard a noise, sounded like a bang and I turned and ran through the shrubbery.'

'Back to the car?'

'No, I didn't, did I? I ran as fast as I could through the woods and back home.'

'What condition was he in when you last saw him?'

'Pissed he was, I told you. He'd been in the pub and then he had more from the bottle in the car, see. I tried to stop him but he wouldn't listen.'

'How was he walking when he went up to the house?'

'Lurching. He made quite a din breaking the window but then he had said he didn't think anyone was in the house, didn't he?'

'Why did you run away?'

'Because I heard the bang, didn't I?'

'One bang or two?'

'Could have been two but if it was more than one I'd turned away and started to run as soon as I heard a bang. I crashed through the shrubbery and fell over once or twice and made quite a bit of noise so I can't rightly say. I'd been watching from some way back. I'd had a few myself. Not like Stevie though. He'd had plenty. Much more than me.'

Mordecai sat down. Vaughan hesitated and then got to his feet.

'You were never in the house?'

'I told you, didn't I? I was back in the shrubbery in the trees.'

'So you can't say what happened after you saw Rouse get through the window?'

'Of course I can't. I wasn't there, was I?'

'You heard a bang–'

'Or two,' said Mordecai.

249

'Yes, yes, or two,' Vaughan said angrily, 'and then you ran away. That's all you tell us, is that right?'

'I've told you all I knows. I didn't go into the house, did I?'

'Did you tell the police all this?'

'I told them I'd been with Stevie in the pub. I said I hadn't been near the house 'cos I hadn't been really near, had I? I was back in the trees.'

'Was Stevie Rouse carrying anything when he went into the house?'

'A torch.'

'How did he break the window?'

'With a stone from the drive.'

'And after he'd got in through the window, you didn't see him again?'

'I told you. I ran back home.'

Vaughan sat down, beckoning to Blake who approached and bent over him.

'I've no further questions,' said Mordecai. Ron Taylor remained in the witness box as his evidence was read over to him, the sheepish grin back on his face. When he had signed the transcript he left the box and Webster escorted him to the back of the court.

'Well,' said Colonel Musgrove, 'any other surprise witnesses?'

Mordecai shook his head. Vaughan was on his feet.

'As I indicated, I suggest the last witness takes the matter no further. He was apparently never even near the house and certainly never entered it. So he cannot help you over what happened when the shooting took place. It is to the unchallenged facts that I ask you to look and I submit that there is ample evidence here to warrant committal for trial on a charge of murder. The accused admits he fired the shot that killed Rouse. The shot that killed Rouse was fired when Rouse had turned away, when he had his back to the accused when he could not be said to be threatening the accused in any way. Even though he was an intruder and had entered the accused's bedroom, nevertheless the use of a pistol, the firing of a deadly weapon that literally blew off the back – and I emphasize the word back – of Rouse's head, was to use wholly disproportionate force in the circumstances of the incident. To shoot, to fire the pistol at that range was a deliberate act of killing. No citizen is entitled to shoot down another except in self-defence and that is only acceptable when that citizen is facing a real and substantial threat to his life. That threat did not arise here. The accused should be sent for trial to answer the charge of murder.'

Vaughan sat down. His manner conveyed that it was all so obvious that he did not think it worth saying more. The prima facie case was there. The evidence was conclusive. All that the magistrates had to do was commit the accused for trial and they could all go home.

'Thank you,' Colonel Musgrove said and took up a card from the papers before him. Francis motioned to Mordecai to stand. Musgrove said, 'I have to read this to you, don't you know. It is laid down. All right?'

Mordecai bowed and Musgrove began to read off the card.

'Do you wish to say anything in answer to the charge? You are not obliged to say anything unless you desire to do so, but whatever you say will be taken down in writing and may be given in evidence upon your trial.'

'I have a submission to make, sir,' said Mordecai. Henry leant down and retrieved the fallen stick. He handed it to Mordecai.

'I was warned that you might,' Musgrove said. 'Go ahead.'

'May it please the bench,' Mordecai began. 'The case that the prosecution has presented in order to show that a prima facie case of murder has been made out so as to warrant my facing trial amounts to this. That at a time when I faced no real threat from the burglar and so was in no need to defend myself, I used a firearm to shoot to kill. I did so, the prosecution claims, at a time when the burglar had turned away to leave the room in which I was lying on the bed. I took up, they say, a pistol that I knew was on the bedside table and in cold blood deliberately shot him in the back of the head. Now you have had

252

read to you Exhibit 4, the statement that I gave to the police – whose conduct, I may add, in this case both before and during these proceedings has been quite deplorable, motivated by malice towards me because of some words I used some months ago to their Chief. Before these proceedings they deliberately alerted a press photographer to my arrest and during them they have even mislaid an exhibit, namely the first bullet, while, you may think, they obviously put their heads together during the luncheon adjournment, all of which reflects little credit on the local force and whatever the result of these proceedings merits serious enquiry.'

He paused, and then went on, 'My account of what actually happened is fully set out in my statement, Exhibit 4. May I repeat the gist of it? I came to the house to pass that night in order to examine the family documents that had been bequeathed to me by my cousin. My statement goes on to say that I had discovered the existence of the pistol when I had gone to bed and after I had read what my cousin, Roderick Fairbairn, had written in those papers of his which were gathered together in Exhibit 5. In those writings he describes how he had acquired that weapon during the last war and how and why he kept it in working order. My statement then explains how it came about that on the night of 25th August, I came across the pistol in the drawer by the bed in which I was sleeping. It also describes how I, who am, as you know, a cripple, was woken and saw in the moonlight from the open window a figure in a balaclava helmet brandishing what we now know is a poker at the foot of the bed where I was lying. Still only half awake and finding as it were the pistol in my hand, I raised it and fired it with the intention of scaring off the intruder.

'My finger must have remained on the trigger and because of the ease of the action of the pistol, two shots were fired in rapid succession. I suggest that the first resulted in the bullet, so inconceivably lost by the incompetence of the local police, lodging in the surround to the door. At this the intruder must have turned and moved away and it was for this reason that the second shot struck the back of his head and killed him.

'As you have also heard from my statement Exhibit 4, I had no intention of shooting at or killing the armed man standing so threateningly at the foot of my bed. I was only half awake; I acted instinctively. I had no intention to kill or to harm. My reaction was the understandable reaction of a man woken from sleep to find a masked and armed figure only a few yards from where he lay. Ronald Taylor, whom the prosecution did not consider worthy of calling, testified to Rouse's intention on that night – to deal with anyone that was in the house, in other words to attack them. Rouse was drunk, he was belligerent, so when he opened the bedroom door he could easily have lurched and staggered, as he had probably fallen about when Taylor saw him break the window and enter the house. That the shot struck the back of his head could have been due to his lurching and staggering when I fired the shots intended to frighten him off.

'These then are the facts. This is the evidence, and I submit that from a proper and fair assessment of this there is no evidence of the crime of murder. A man died, yes, from a bullet to his head fired by myself, but that does not mean there is any evidence that warrants the conclusion that the person who pulled that trigger must undergo a trial on a charge of murder. It is not a case where a person deliberately keeps to hand an unlawfully possessed weapon and uses it deliberately, intending to kill or maim. No evidence has been submitted that would allow you to hold that the prosecution has made out a prima facie case of deliberate murder sufficient for you to commit me to stand trial.'

Mordecai paused. He looked deliberately at the magistrates, first at the chairman and then at the two other magistrates on either side of him. 'This,' he said slowly, 'was death by misadventure, nothing less, nothing more.

The death by misadventure of a drunken, belligerent burglar who had, as perhaps you may think he had done many times before, broken into a house in the middle of the night, threatening and terrorizing persons asleep in their beds. And it was through misadventure and misadventure alone that he received the awful consequences for what he was doing.' Mordecai paused again. The sweat was running from his forehead and he was swaying on his feet, supported by his two sticks held before him.

'I ask you to rule therefore that the prosecution have failed to make out a prima facie case of murder and I invite you to discharge me.'

There was dead silence in the court. Henry put up a hand to steady Mordecai as he subsided into his seat.

'Thank you,' Musgrove said and he gathered together the papers on his desk. 'The bench will now retire to consider the evidence and the submission.'

With that, the magistrates disappeared.

The court burst into a crash of sound as, with Elizabeth and Webster following behind them, Mordecai and Henry made their way through the crowd of spectators to the robing room.

Gwyn Vaughan, who during Mordecai's submission had sat smiling complacently and now and then shaking his head, remained in his place at the advocates' table. He began to leaf through the files that he had brought with him in his briefcase. Francis stood chatting to the usher and other court officials but watching Vaughan.

Some of the spectators had left to stretch their legs in the street outside; others remained where they were, so as not to lose their places when the magistrates returned. After a few minutes, and seeing that Vaughan was busy with his files, Francis gathered up his papers and, announcing loudly that he was going to his office, ostentatiously left the court through the side doors. Once in his office, however, he slipped down the corridor to the judge's room which the magistrates were using and knocked on the door.

'Is there anything I can get you?' he asked as he entered. 'Tea or coffee?'

Musgrove and Southern shook their heads. Mrs Whitfield was absent. Francis lingered in the open door. 'Is Mrs Whitfield all right?' he asked.

'In the loo,' said the Colonel.

'I shall be in my room should you need anything,' Francis said. He still remained where he was. He saw Mrs Whitfield coming up the corridor. 'Ah, here she is,' he said.

Mrs Whitfield gave him a smile, which he didn't return.

'I'm sorry about the police officers having lunch together,' he said. 'I hadn't expected that.' The door of the room still remained open behind him.

'Damn fools,' said the Colonel. 'But it don't affect the evidence of the killing.'

'Of course they talked about the case,' Southern added. 'Stands to reason they would. And what was all that about the photographer at the arrest at eight o'clock in the morning in London?'

'It's the evidence about the killing that matters,' the Colonel said. Francis still did not leave. Musgrove walked to the window. 'The man's head,' he went on. 'That weapon made a terrible mess to the back of that fellow's head.'

'What did you think of Mr Ledbury's speech?' said Mrs Whitfield brightly.

No one replied. Francis said, 'Well, I shall be in my room down the corridor if you think I can help over anything. Perhaps you'd let me know when you've decided.'

He began to leave but then came back. 'There is one other thing you should know. If you were to discharge the accused, it is not like an acquittal in an actual trial when an accused may never be tried again for that offence. Where magistrates have refused to commit, the prosecution can, if they think it right, apply to the judge for a bill of indictment and the accused has to stand trial even though the magistrates have discharged him.'

'So even if we discharge the fellow, the prosecution can still go after him?' asked the Colonel.

'That is correct. It might depend on whether the bench had expressed any opinion about the prosecution. I imagine that in those circumstances it would be doubtful if the prosecution would dare to seek a bill from the judge.'

'I see. Thank you for reminding us of that.' Musgrove walked to the window. 'Those photographs that showed what was left of Rouse's head reminded me of the war.'

Francis was still by the door, waiting.

'Well, thank you, Francis,' said the Colonel. 'We'll knock on your door when we're ready.'

In the advocates' robing room, Mordecai was finishing the second half-bottle of champagne. 'At least the prosecution didn't make much about the empties they found in the kitchen of the house,' he said.

No one replied. Then Mordecai said to Henry, 'If they commit me for trial, be sure you ask for bail to be renewed. If they refuse, send for Terence Brady and get him to apply to the judge.'

Henry nodded. He remembered how

surprised Terence had been to learn that Mordecai had demanded a full-scale committal. When Henry had spoken with him on the telephone the night before last Terence had said again, 'Of course I don't know the details of the evidence, but the magistrates are certain to send him for trial, especially if Leslie Harrison is presiding. But whether Mordecai's later convicted by a jury, that's another matter.' The law, Terence said, was pretty clear. He surely could not expect to win a discharge at committal.

'It's what Mordecai wants,' Henry had replied.

But at least they had the luck to have had Colonel Musgrove and not Leslie Harrison. With Harrison they'd not have had a chance. Why, Henry wondered, had Harrison not sat? And the other two? He knew little about them. Of course they could outvote the maverick Colonel.

In the robing room they now sat in silence. None felt there was anything more to be said. Webster was seated on a hard, wooden chair, his knees apart, looking at the ground; Henry was fiddling with his papers making sure that he had Terence Brady's telephone number and checking the dates of the next assize. Mordecai had finished the champagne and lay back in his chair, his eyes again closed. Elizabeth watched him. The minutes passed. After half an hour there came a knock on the door. Webster jumped up and opened it. It was the usher.

'Mr Peyton says that the magistrates are ready to come back into court.'

Already? It's too soon, thought Henry. They are coming back too soon. They hadn't been out for under an hour. A short retirement, he knew, is rarely good news for the defence.

They re-formed their procession led by Mordecai on his two sticks, and he and Henry went to their places by the advocates' table in the well of the court. Vaughan was already there. Elizabeth and Webster slipped into their seats at the side.

Mordecai remained standing. Francis Peyton came through the side door and took his place below the bench. The curtain across the door behind the bench was drawn by the usher and the court rose as the magistrates entered and took their seats.

'Please remain standing,' Francis said to Mordecai.

From her place Elizabeth kept her eyes on Mordecai. His head was bowed, the few strands of dark hair plastered across the top. A vein was throbbing on the side of his face and there was sweat on his forehead. She had not forgotten his fear of prison.

Colonel Musgrove looked round the court, cleared his throat and began to read from a piece of paper.

'This is an unusual case and quite unlike many other committals for trial,' he began. 'We have listened with great care to the evidence, and first we want to express our regret at some of the conduct and attitude of the local police, not only at the time of the arrest but even during these proceedings. We consider that it was below the usual standard of the county force and we invite the authorities to look into it.'

He looked round the court as though searching for the two police officers. But they were seated far to the back. He cleared his throat again.

'That, however, does not affect the facts of the case we've been considering, none of which are in dispute. A young man was killed by the accused who shot him with a pistol. The whole of the back of his head was blown off. It was a large .45 calibre pistol which is, I might add, a particularly powerful weapon.' He paused. 'The deceased was a criminal. He had broken into the house and he may have made a practice of breaking into and entering local households and terrorizing householders hereabouts. He had earlier in the evening, when he had been drinking heavily, declared that if he found anybody in the house he would, to use the phrase of the witness Mr Taylor, "deal with" them.

'In this instance he broke into this isolated

house in which the accused, who happens to be a–' he cleared his throat – 'a cripple, was spending the night. The accused woke to find a masked burglar armed with a weapon that turned out to be a poker, standing at the foot of his bed. There was no light – that is no artificial light – only the light of the moon. The accused stretched to pick up his torch but instead his hand landed on a pistol that he had come across earlier in the night. As he said in his statement to the police, he was half awake at the time and he fired it in order to scare off the burglar who he thought was going to attack him. He had no intention, he said in his statement, of hitting the fellow but in fact he did.'

Another pause, another glance around the court. 'In our opinion the death of this young–'

'Burglar,' prompted Southern quietly.

'Yes, thank you. The death of this young burglar was brought about by his own criminal behaviour and amounted, in our opinion, which we believe is a common-sense opinion, to what has been aptly described as death by misadventure.'

Once again the Colonel paused and looked around the court and his glance fell this time on Gwyn Vaughan sitting at the table below him.

'Frankly, and with due respect to the prosecuting authorities,' he went on, laying down the paper from which he had been reading, 'we are surprised that a prosecution alleging murder was ever commenced.'

Vaughan, his hands clasped before him on the table, looked up at the bench angrily. Then you didn't listen to what I said, he thought. I told you what this prosecution was about.

The chairman continued, 'The death of this young thief was, as I said, death by misadventure and the prosecution has failed to establish that there is a prima facie case of murder that this accused is required to answer.'

A noise broke out in the court like a great gust of wind rustling the leaves of a tree – or as if, as Elizabeth thought, the whole court had uttered a communal sigh. One or two spectators at the back of the court clapped.

'Silence,' shouted the usher.

'Accordingly,' the Colonel concluded, 'we discharge the accused.'

A hubbub of noise arose, including more clapping. Reporters began an immediate scramble from the press box and pushed their way out. 'Silence,' called the usher again, 'silence.'

'Well, that's that,' said Colonel Musgrove cheerily, gathering together his papers. 'The court is adjourned.'

When the three magistrates disappeared through the door at the back of the bench, pandemonium broke out. The clapping was now universal and some even cheered. Henry put his arm around Mordecai, who stood with his head bowed. Elizabeth ran to him and kissed his cheek. People began to crowd around him, trying to slap him on the back, and Webster had to push them away. Francis intervened and showed Mordecai, followed by Elizabeth, Henry and Webster, through the side door to his office. 'I'll fetch you when the crowd has dispersed,' he said.

'It's over, Mordecai,' said Elizabeth. 'It's over at last. Now you can come and stay the night with us at Pemberley.'

'No, my dear. It is not over,' said Mordecai. 'Thank you, you are very kind but tonight I would rather be alone so I shall go back to London. Threadgold will be very angry. He will ask the judge for a bill of indictment.'

In the judge's room Musgrove was putting on his light overcoat. 'Thank you both for your help,' he said to the others. 'I hope we did the right thing. A bit unusual, but no harm in that.'

'No question we did the right thing,' said Southern. 'Whatever the law may say, they shouldn't have prosecuted him for murder. A cripple threatened by a man in a mask in the middle of the night in a deserted house with no telephone! Where's the justice in prosecuting him for murder? It wasn't as if he had come armed to the house. He found the pistol there. The police are far too ready to jump on decent citizens. They should spend more time chasing criminals.' He paused and then said, 'I didn't tell you but recently I had a run-in with them over my young son.'

'I didn't know that,' said Musgrove. Francis remained silent.

'Yes,' went on Southern. 'They pulled him in with some of his mates for making a noise outside a restaurant. No one had complained. A damn side too heavy-handed, I thought.'

'I suspect there was something personal behind the prosecution of Ledbury,' said Musgrove. 'Remember all that about the Chief Constable?' Southern nodded. The Colonel went on, 'Ledbury's probably a damned awkward cuss.' He shook his head. 'But we couldn't send him to a trial for the murder of a burglar on that evidence.' He broke into a chuckle. 'Three empty bottles of champagne! I liked that.'

I thought you would, Francis said to himself.

Detective Sergeant West walked with Chief Superintendent Blake to their car. 'A cock-up,' he said. 'I had a hunch it might be.'

'Shut up,' Blake replied savagely.

A little later Elizabeth drove away. Webster had returned with the car and helped Mordecai into the back seat. 'Well done, sir,' he said, 'well done. That's finished then.'

'No,' said Mordecai. 'They can still apply to the judge for a bill of indictment.'

'They wouldn't dare,' said Webster as they drove off.

'Oh yes, the Director of Public Prosecutions would,' said Mordecai. He added, 'I'm very tired. So I shall sleep.'

In the robing room Vaughan, seething with indignation, telephoned the Director in Buckingham Gate. The Deputy Director, Robert Walker, was with Threadgold in his room.

At first Threadgold refused to believe what he was being told. He ordered Vaughan to repeat what the magistrate had said. Then he became incandescent.

'It's an outrage, a scandal. The committal should have been a formality. The decision was blatantly perverse.'

Vaughan for a third time repeated what Colonel Musgrove had said about the prosecution. 'How dare he!' Threadgold burst out. 'The impertinence! The prosecution was entirely proper. It was in the public interest that Ledbury should be prosecuted.'

Still holding the receiver in his hand, he

removed his pince-nez from his nose and then jammed it on again. Walker, fascinated, saw the reddened skin left by the spectacles on the bridge of the Director's nose.

'The Lord Chancellor should see to it that those magistrates are dismissed.' He looked up at Walker. 'You've heard what happened?'

Walker nodded. 'That they've discharged Ledbury? Yes.'

Threadgold barked into the receiver, 'Find Roland Gibbs immediately. Tell him to speak to me urgently. We must apply to the judge for a bill. I will not permit so important a prosecution to be railroaded by a pack of country jack-asses.'

A clerk came into the room with a piece of paper. 'This has just come through on the tape, sir,' the clerk said. 'It's the full report of what was said at Dilminster.' Threadgold snatched it, read it and passed it to Walker.

When he had read it, Walker said, 'I see it says that the decision was greeted with much applause.' He paused. 'In view of what the chairman said in dismissing the charge, might it not be difficult to apply to the judge for a bill?'

'No. We shall apply tomorrow, at the very latest.' Threadgold again barked into the telephone, 'Are you still there, Vaughan? Well, find Gibbs tonight and tell him to apply to the presiding judge first thing in the morning.'

In Dilminster Francis offered Mrs Whitfield a lift home. When they were in the car, she said, 'Was that what you expected?'

'What I hoped for.'

They were silent for a time. Then she said, 'You handpicked us. You chose all three of us.'

'I did.'

'You chose Colonel Musgrove in preference to Sir Leslie because the Colonel is more of a maverick?'

'More likely to do justice, you mean.'

'And you knew that Brian Southern had a run-in with the police about his son?'

'I did.'

'And you chose me, because I knew what had happened when you and Barbara were attacked in Ealing by those villains and what they did to Barbara.'

'Yes.'

There was another silence. 'So you got the result you wanted?'

'It was the result that I knew was right.'

'Right in law – or because of what happened to you and Barbara in Ealing?' He did not reply and she went on, 'You once told me that when the men broke in on that awful night demanding money and you heard them hitting and beating Barbara, you'd have killed them if you could.'

'I would have – if I'd had the chance.'

'But you didn't have a gun.' He did not reply.

She stared out of the window of the car. 'It was the start of all Barbara's trouble,' she said. 'It destroyed her.'

'It destroyed our life together.'

'Poor Barbara,' said Mrs Whitfield. Mordecai Ledbury, she thought. You have been the beneficiary of what Barbara has suffered.

Back in his office Walker telephoned Brett, the Legal Secretary in the Law Officers' Department. Brett too had seen the tape on the proceedings at Dilminster. 'The Director,' Walker said, 'has given instructions for Gibbs QC to apply tomorrow to the judge for a bill.'

'But you've read what the bench said about the prosecution? The press will be up in arms.'

'I know,' Walker replied gloomily. 'But he's adamant. Will you inform the Attorney?'

'He's in the House,' Brett replied, 'dealing with a very tricky adjournment debate about an extradition case. I won't be able to speak to him until later.'

Others too had learnt what the magistrates had said at Dilminster and the public reaction to the decision, O'Halloran, the press secretary at No. 10, in particular. He spoke to Brett at the Attorney's office and then switched on the six o'clock news on

TV. The commentator described the scenes of enthusiasm when the magistrates announced their decision. He telephoned Miles, the editor of the *Daily News*, an old friend with whom he'd formerly worked as a journalist. 'What's the press reaction to the Dilminster case?' he enquired.

After a few minutes' conversation, O'Halloran rang another friend, the editor of the *Daily Journal*, one of the broadsheets that supported the administration. The press reaction was confirmed. Unanimous approval of what the magistrates had done. But, O'Halloran was told, there was a rumour that the government was trying to get a bill of indictment to overthrow the magistrates' decision. 'But it's not the government,' he wailed. 'It's not us. It's the prosecuting authorities.'

He put a call through to the Lord Chancellor's Department.

'About the Dilminster case,' he began.

'Ah, yes,' said Sir Gervase, 'I have heard the result. All wrong in law, of course, but wholly understandable.'

'I'm told the DPP now wishes to apply to a judge for a bill of indictment and–'

'That would be very foolish,' Sir Gervase interrupted. 'He should leave well alone.'

'I quite agree and I was wondering if the Lord Chancellor–'

'Good heavens, no. It's nothing to do with

the Lord Chancellor. It's not a matter for him. It's not a matter for interference by any political minister either.'

'But if the DPP goes ahead, the government will be blamed and the press—'

'My dear boy, remember your history, if you were taught any. The Campbell case in the 1920s. The whole government was brought down because it was thought ministers had interfered in a prosecution. No, no, my dear boy, this is solely a matter for the Attorney General. It's his business and no one else's.'

Sir Gervase rang off. Pity he had to give that advice, he thought. If the government were to fall, he'd be rid of his obstreperous Lord Chancellor.

O'Halloran sent for a car and was driven to the House of Commons where he went to see the Chief Whip.

'If they try and reverse the magistrates,' said the Chief Whip, 'the government will be blamed and the whole media pack will be at our throats. We're in enough trouble with them as it is. We couldn't possibly survive.'

'I'm told that only the Attorney can do anything,' said O'Halloran.

'And he's on the bench in the House.'

The Chief Whip thought for a moment. 'I'll see if I can have a tactful word with Smythe, the Solicitor.'

A quarter of an hour later Philip Smythe,

the Solicitor General, joined the Whip on duty on the Treasury Bench inside the Chamber. 'How's it going?' he whispered to the Whip.

'Terrible,' the Whip groaned. 'They're tearing strips off the Attorney.'

Smythe slipped past him and took a seat next to the Attorney. Herbert Meadows, his face pale, was taking notes on a clipboard. He turned his head and said wanly, 'It's very tricky, Philip. In fact it's very nasty. They are being quite poisonous. I've never experienced anything like this before.'

An Opposition backbencher who had been speaking, suddenly sat down, shaking his finger accusingly at the Attorney as he did so.

'There's a problem at Dilminster,' Smythe whispered, 'and the Chief Whip–'

'Sir George Hendricks,' called the Speaker, and the Shadow Attorney General rose from the Opposition front bench. 'The conduct of the Right Honourable Gentleman the Attorney General over this matter,' he began, 'has been little short of scandalous.'

'About Dilminster,' Smythe whispered again.

'No, no,' said Herbert Meadows. 'Not now. I can't deal with Dilminster until I have replied to Hendricks. I must listen to what he has to say. Later, later, about Dilminster.'

The Chief Whip was waiting behind the

Speaker's chair. Smythe shook his head. 'He says, later. He can't talk now.'

The Chief Whip swung on his heel with an oath. 'The matter has to be settled this evening. Tomorrow will be too late.'

From his room Smythe tried to locate the Director. Threadgold was at a discussion evening at the Athenaeum. He was not pleased to be called to the telephone.

'The Attorney wants to speak to you,' Smythe began. 'About Dilminster.'

'The matter is in hand, Solicitor,' Threadgold replied testily. 'My man in the West Country will be seeing Roland Gibbs tomorrow morning. He will apply to the judge for a bill. We'll soon have it sorted out.'

'The Attorney wants to have a word with you–'

'Tell him not to worry. I have it all in hand. I'm in the middle of what we call a "talk evening", you understand, and I wish to participate. Goodnight, Solicitor.'

The Chief Whip tried to find the Lord Chancellor.

'He's left for a reception in the City,' said Sir Gervase. 'Can I help?'

'It's about Dilminster,' said the Chief Whip.

'Ah, yes.' Sir Gervase did not try to conceal the note of satisfaction in his voice. 'No. 10 has already been on. I hear that the DPP is intent on obtaining a bill from the

274

judge. In my opinion that would be very foolish.'

'It's nothing to do with us but the press will blame us,' said the Chief Whip bitterly.

'They will,' Sir Gervase replied cheerfully.

'How can he be stopped?'

'Not by me and certainly not by you. No, only the Attorney can do that. If he's got the balls, that is, to overrule the Director. But if it ever gets out that you had a hand in stopping it, there'll be the devil to pay. The government would come crashing about your ears.' He laughed happily. Would that it would, he thought. 'So don't you speak to the Attorney,' he went on. 'Hendricks is very experienced. If he discovered you'd got yourself involved, he'd soon have the place by the ears. He's no softie.' Sir Gervase laughed again. 'I must be off now.'

The Chief Whip cursed again and poured himself a stiff whisky and soda. The trouble is, he thought morosely, Meadows is just what Hendricks is not. A softie.

In the chamber the Attorney was struggling to make himself heard in reply to Hendricks' blistering attack. A barrage of noise came from the Opposition benches and Meadows was interrupted continuously and fiercely. His natural courtesy made him give way to the interrupters. He shouldn't let them, thought the Whip on duty. He shouldn't let them. It's quite unnecessary.

Philip Smythe had returned to the Treasury bench to show his support for the Attorney. At last Herbert concluded his speech and sank back beside Philip on the Bench. 'A very lame effort,' the Whip on duty noted in his report. The division was called and members flocked into the chamber from the dining rooms. In the division lobby the Chief Whip bustled past Herbert. 'A very difficult debate,' Herbert called out. The Chief Whip merely nodded and passed on.

The government majority was three, and that was only because the plane bringing four Opposition members back from Strasbourg was held up by fog. Meadows knew that he had not done well. As a rule he was able to handle the House, which usually accepted his mild and agreeable style. But tonight had been different and Hendricks had been devastatingly offensive. In the Attorney's room he flopped exhausted into his chair.

'Dilminster,' Philip began.

'Yes, Dilminster,' he said absently, 'Dilminster. What's happened at Dilminster?'

Philip told him, repeating what the magistrates had said in discharging Mordecai and describing the applause with which it had been greeted. 'Did they?' the Attorney replied. 'I always wondered, as a man you understand, not as a lawyer, whether it was

276

right to charge Ledbury with murder. But the Director was very insistent.'

Philip went on to tell him about the Director's intention to apply the next day to the judge for a bill. He added that any attempt to reverse the magistrates would be met with violent public objection. The press was united in approval of the magistrates. Obtaining a bill would be immensely unpopular. The government would be blamed and the press would turn on them without mercy. Indeed the government might fall.

'Oh dear,' said the Attorney, 'oh dear.'

The Director had enjoyed the discussion at the Athenaeum, which had been devoted to Italian Literature. He himself had made what he considered was an elegant and witty contribution about Giuseppe di Lampedusa and whether Don Fabrizio was an autobiographical portrait. No one had laughed or even smiled but the Director was satisfied with his contribution. It was erudite and amusing, he told himself.

The evening was fine, he needed a breath of air, and he walked back to his flat in Gray's Inn. As he entered the telephone rang.

'Is that you, Director?' Threadgold recognized the voice.

'It is, Attorney.'

'I have been trying to get in touch with you but–'

'I have been at my club.'

'I know. I missed you. I hope you had an agreeable evening.'

'Very agreeable, thank you.'

'When I telephoned they said you'd just left.' The Attorney hesitated and then went on, 'But the matter was urgent and I couldn't delay. I wanted you to know that I have issued a statement to the Press Association.'

'Indeed, Attorney, and what about?'

'Perhaps I'd better read it to you.'

'Please do.'

The Attorney cleared his throat and began to read. 'The Attorney General has received a full report of the proceedings of the Dilminster magistrates court when Mr Mordecai Ledbury was discharged by the magistrates as having no case to answer on the charge that he had murdered a burglar. The Attorney General has reviewed the evidence given in those proceedings and noted what was said by the magistrates in discharging the accused. He has decided that no further action will be taken with regard to this prosecution and that no application will be made for a bill of indictment.'

The Attorney paused. 'That is the statement that has been issued.' There was silence. 'Are you there, Director?'

'I am.'

'Well, that's what's been done. I'm sure it's for the best. The PA has the statement. I thought you should know.'

Again there was silence. Then the Director said, 'Then, of course, I resign. Goodnight,' and he slammed down the receiver.

'Oh dear,' said the Attorney.

It was a slow drive to London. It had begun to rain and there was an accident on the eastbound carriageway of the A303: an overturned lorry and a multiple pile-up of several cars. So they were stationary for a good hour. Later the traffic into London was horrendous.

Mordecai slept most of the time and when awake kept silent. Webster asked and got permission to switch on the car radio to get information about the traffic. The general news bulletin reported the result of the Dilminster proceedings and what the magistrates had said when discharging the accused. The comment in the press and their opposition to any further proceedings was quoted. John Plater and the *Daily News* were playing their part.

Some hours later they pulled in to Albany. As Webster carried in Mordecai's bag, Mordecai said, 'I am very grateful. You have been a tower of strength.'

'Glad to have been a help,' Webster replied

cheerily as he left. 'They should never have started it.'

But they had, Mordecai thought as he entered his rooms. And who, he thought, could blame them if they had known what he knew.

The telephone rang. It was Henry. He read the Attorney's statement over the telephone. 'Thank you,' said Mordecai, 'thank you. We'll speak again tomorrow.'

So it really was over. He sat in his chair staring into the empty grate, remembering all that had really happened that night at Water Meadow House. First the long hours in the musty library and his discovery of the story of his mother's past. Then the lights on the ground floor failing, his climb up the stairs using the torch and his struggle to get into the high four-poster bed. And his finding the pistol.

What had happened next he had not told. Not the truth, that is. Not all the truth. In his statement to the police and his submission, his speech to the magistrates, he had told of waking suddenly to find the intruder at the foot of the bed and of when half awake stretching out his hand which fell on the pistol and of his firing wildly, not to kill or hurt but to scare the man who was threatening him. None of that had been under formal oath as a witness for he had never been required to and had never spoken on oath.

But the statement and the submission were not the real truth.

For he had been woken not by the man entering his room but by the sound of the breaking of glass, coming from the ground floor. Immediately he had thought of what Henry had told him – that on the night of Roderick Fairbairn's death, someone had been in the house. Now someone was in the house once again.

Wide awake he had reached out for the pistol that he had put on the bedside table. He sat up in the bed with the pistol in one hand, the torch in the other, ready and waiting. He heard the footsteps climbing the stairs. They stopped on the landing outside the bedroom door and he raised the pistol. In the moonlight he saw clearly the handle of the door slowly turning, the door opening and a figure framed on the threshold. Immediately he had switched on the torch. The beam fell on a man in a black balaclava mask and he could see the man's eyes glinting in the slits of the mask. The man raised an arm, shading his eyes. Then with an oath he lurched and turned. Mordecai had taken aim – and fired. One shot. For a time he lay on the bed, the pistol still in his hands, thinking of the morning and when the police would come. They would find a man shot dead by Mordecai Ledbury. And they would be the Dilminster police who would be very happy to investigate a killing by Mordecai Ledbury. He remembered Henry's warning about the Chief Constable, and the judge's dinner party and the Chief Constable's provocative wife and what he had said about the police. He could not expect them to be very friendly.

It was a shooting, and it was a shooting by him, no question about that. He'd have to admit that. So it would have to be an excusable shooting, a shooting in self-defence. Of that he would have to make sure.

Slowly he had slipped his legs over the side of the bed and examined the dead man. He saw that it was the back of the head that the bullet had struck, when the man had turned away. For a time he had stood there thinking. Then, still in his pyjamas, he went down to the library. He took the poker from the fireplace and laboriously clambered back up the stairs. He wiped it carefully with his silk handkerchief to ensure that there were none of his fingerprints upon it, and holding the poker still wrapped in the handkerchief, he had placed it in the right hand of the dead man. Then he removed the handkerchief. He decided that if he had fired when half awake and in panic to scare away the intruder, it would be more convincing if he had fired two shots. One that had missed and one that had killed. So he lay back on the bed and taking aim fired the second shot into the lintel of the door.

That had been the risk over Ronald Taylor's evidence. For Taylor, waiting in the trees, said that at the sound of a shot he had turned and run, crashing through the shrubbery. And the second shot had been some time after the first and Taylor could not have heard that. So he had to take the risk of suggesting to Taylor that in his rush to get away he might not have heard the second. And Taylor had accepted it.

Having put the poker in the dead man's hand and fired the second shot, he had dressed and at first light gone downstairs and taken up position seated by the hall table, to await the arrival of Webster – and the police.

He thought of Roderick Fairbairn who had died near to where he was now sitting, near the flowers that he apparently used to place in the vase in the hall in honour of his dead love. Henry had said he'd been told that someone was in the house when Roderick Fairbairn had died, and that the shock of seeing the intruder could have brought on the massive heart attack that killed him. And the intruder who had caused the death of Roderick Fairbairn was, like as not (and confirmed later by Taylor although not known to Mordecai as he sat waiting), the

283

man in the mask now lying dead on the landing outside the bedroom. The man Mordecai had shot. The man he had intended to kill – and he had killed.

Mordecai rose now from his chair in his rooms in Albany and went to the bathroom. He took the small bottle of capsules from his pocket – the capsules he would have taken had the case gone against him. He had got them when Harriet was dying, to help her had the pain become so intolerable that she wished to die. But in the end she had gone back to her son in Northumbria to die at his home.

He replaced the small bottle at the back of the cabinet. For use, he thought grimly, another time.

Now he opened a bottle of champagne and went back to his chair and thought again of Water Meadow House and the malign spell it had cast over the life of his mother – and then over himself. He had no regrets at what he had done. He thought of it as an act guarding his heritage. He had been defending his house. And when he had, he then knew what it was to kill – like so many in the long line of his ancestors.

While Mordecai sat in his room at Albany remembering what had happened that night, Stevie Rouse's elder brother, Jim, was making his way through the tangle of under-growth surrounding Water Meadow House. When he reached the house he found the window through which Stevie had broken in. He had with him a small can and when half an hour later he left the house by the window through which he had entered, the fire had taken hold. By the time he reached the car and set out for the coast, he could see above the trees that the place was ablaze.

By morning nothing was left of Water Meadow House in which so many gener-ations of Fairbairns had lived and died and in which Stevie Rouse too had met his end. Of its contents all that remained were those family papers that had been removed by Mordecai and taken to his chambers in Albany and which told the story of the childhood of Alice Fairbairn; and the file of Roderick Fairbairn's writings that had been used as an exhibit in the Ledbury committal proceedings. Over the subsequent years that exhibit gathered dust in the basement of the office of the Director of Public Prosecutions in Buckingham Gate. There it had been added to the more bulky file labelled R. v. Ledbury which marked the end of the long reign in office of Director Threadgold.

One other exhibit from the committal pro-ceedings also survived and it was retained in the armoury of the Dilminster police. This was the pistol, the relic of war that the young officer, Roderick Fairbairn, had purchased from the elderly gunsmith in St James's Street long, long ago, on a summer afternoon before the bombs began to fall on London.

This Large Print Book, for people
who cannot read normal print,
is published under the auspices of

THE ULVERSCROFT FOUNDATION